The Guardian Angel

Lou Baker

Contents

Chapter 1

S tiles POVI pulled into the long driveway that led up to the Hale house. Derek finally rebuilt it, he added on rooms. It's huge. Twice the size it was before. He says we'll need it for when "the pack expands" but honestly, I think it's a little much.

It's three stories, all of the bedrooms are soundproof because nobody really wants to listen to werewolf sex, there is a bathroom connected to each and every bedroom, plus two extra, the kitchen is one out of a hallmark movie and there's a big enough dining room it looks like a conference hall. He also added a library in and a pool in the back.

I walked inside throwing my jacket on the railing of the staircase and walked into the kitchen. Nobody was home. Huh, home. This isn't home. This doesn't feel like home. I'm eighteen, I shouldn't have to live on my own. I guess I'm not really on my own but this isn't my house. But a part time job and college debt don't pay the bills and I can't handle everything that comes with adulthood alone right now.

I still think back to the end of senior year, my dad knew all about the pack, about the supernatural. He always wanted to help. I never thought I'd lose him. But I did. I lost myself when he passed. It's not like the pack needs me anyway. I'm human. I'm a weak, pathetic human.

My chest tightened as I tried to hold back the tears that were urging their way out.

"Stiles.." I heard softly behind me. It was Derek. I hated when it was Derek. Not because I hate him or anything. It's the opposite. But he can't know that. I won't let him know that. It's not like he'd like me back.

"Stiles, what's wrong?" I felt his hand hook itself to the small of my back.

"Nothing." I got out, my voice cracking.

"You can talk to me." He said.

"There's nothing to talk about!" I snapped looking at him. "I'm sorry." My voice got drastically quieter as I wiped my face.

"I know what you're going through." He said softly.

"I don't want to talk about it." I moved away from him going upstairs.

I don't know why I get so angry around him. I'm an emotional roller coaster. One second I'm screaming at him, the next I'm crying on his shoulder. I don't know how he still puts up with me. I don't even want to put up with me anymore.

Later that night I dragged myself from my room to meet the pack for our weekly meeting. I didn't even care at this point. I'm not going to be allowed to fight. They don't ever let me fight. I'm too weak, I'm human, I could get hurt.

I sat next to Scott. "You okay?" He asked, patting my knee.

"Fine."

I zoned out throughout the meeting. It wasn't important to me anyways. I watched as the pack joked around with each other.

Scott, Isaac, Lydia, and Allison were laughing about something, pushing each other in a joking manner. Jackson, Danny, and Ethan were talking in the corner of the living room. Erica, Boyd, and Aiden were watching tv complaining about what was happening together. Cora was scolding Derek who obviously wasn't listening. Instead he was staring at me.

I raised my eyebrow to him getting the same response back. I rolled my eyes seeing him smirk. Cora hit him and yelled because he wasn't paying attention.

"Stiles!" Scott yelled. I turned to look at him. "You wanna play a game with us?" He asked.

I shook my head getting up and walking to the porch.

Derek POV

I watched Stiles walk outside. I shook my head turning to Cora.

"Shut up."

Her face scrunched up in anger.

"Don't tell me what to do you asshole." She said punching me. I rolled my eyes following in the direction Stiles went.

He was sitting on the porch steps, cigarette resting between his fingers.

"Why are you smoking?" I asked.

He blew out a puff of smoke. "We all have our reasons." He mumbled.

"You shouldn't." I sat next to him, "It's not going to do anything good for you."

"Why do you drink? You don't get any side effects from it." He shot back.

I sighed staring out into the woods. "I don't get you anymore.."

He didn't reply.

"I know you're dealing with a lot but shutting everyone out isn't going to make it any better. Trust me."

"Talking about it won't bring him back." Stiles snapped.

I grabbed the rest of the pack of cigarettes he had sitting next to him on the porch crushing it in my hand. "Stop smoking." I begged standing up and beginning to walk inside.

"It helps...it helps me forget. For just a few minutes it distracts me. I don't know what else to do, Derek." I heard is voice crack.

I sighed, "I'm always going to be here for you....when you want to talk."

He nodded, mumbling a "not today." and putting out his cigarette. He walked past me and back inside.

I wish he would just open up. I hate seeing him like this.

Chapter 2

S tiles POV

The pack was sitting out front of the Hale house. I could hear them from the living room. I should probably go outside with them. At least pretend I'm trying to not mope around. But all I want to do is cry. I don't even contribute to the pack in any way so what's the point? I don't even know why I'm "part of the pack" anymore.

I sighed and pushed myself up off the couch and headed for the front door. As I walked out I could see most of the pack was playing tag or something. Derek and Boyd were off to the side talking to each other. I sat on the steps watching everyone else. I didn't even notice Derek came over to sit by me.

"Hey." He said, making me jump.

"Hi."

"You okay?"

"I'm trying to be." I said feeling a lump form in my throat.

"We're all here for you." He said. I nodded, looking away from him.

"Yeah, once pack, always pack." I looked up to see Isaac.

"Thanks." I mumbled, digging a stick into the dirt.

Isaac asked Derek something making the Alpha get up. Not having his presence next to me kind of hurt. He makes everything hurt a little less. I sighed seeing Isaac and Derek back by Boyd. All three of them talking for awhile before Boyd walked off with Erica and Isaac went back with the rest of the pack.

Somethings not right though. It feels...off. I looked around the trees. I started to feel at ease. Nothing showing up until I heard what sounded like a bow and arrow being shot. But Allison's not here. Who would it be?

My eyes locked onto the person and soon onto the arrow.

"DEREK!" I yelled getting up faster than I ever thought possible. I ran into Derek actually pushing him to the ground.

Derek POV

"DEREK!" I heard Stiles scream. I turned just as he pushed me to the ground.

"What was that for?" I asked. He got this pained look on his face as he tried to get up.

"Stiles." I said quietly. "Oh my god. Stop moving." An arrow was sticking out of his side.

"He's in the trees." His voice was barely audible as he sat on the ground.

"Shit. S-Scott get me a towel...and uh..." I couldn't get my words out. Scott ran inside without without a thought.

"I'm gonna pull it out." I told Stiles seeing the boy shake his head.

"No, it hurts." He cried laying down.

"Stiles, I have to." I said as the pack started gathering around. "I have to." I was trying not to cry.

"You have to stay awake bud." I heard Scott as he set the stuff down. Stiles managed a small groan in response.

"Fuck." I snapped to myself. I placed my hand on his side to pull out some of the pain. I grabbed onto the arrow hissing in pain as it burnt my skin.

"Fuck." I shouted pulling it out and tossing it to the side. I looked at my hand seeing it was bleeding.

"Son of a bitch." I groaned. "Stiles, stay awake."

His heartbeat grew faint as I started stitching up his side.

"Stiles, come on. Wake up." The pack was quiet.

By the time I finished his heartbeat was barely there.

"He's not going to make it...is he?" Isaac asked.

"Where the fuck did that guy go?" I said, trying to pull out more of his pain.

"Boyd and Erica went after him." Isaac told me.

"Stiles, wake up." I heard Scott cry.

Isaac POV

"Fuck!" Derek yelled getting up. He rubbed his hands over his face. "It should've been me." He mumbled.

"That arrow wouldn't even hurt you why would he push you out of the way?" I asked.

"With how much wolfsbane it was soaked in I would've been dead in minutes." Derek said forcing himself not to cry. "FUCK!" He screamed again before running off.

"Stiles, please wake up." Scott cried.

"Scott he's gone." Lydia said trying to pull him away from Stiles.

"No!" Scott yelled.

I felt Danny come up behind me and pull me into a hug. Derek was inside breaking things, yelling, crying. Erica and Boyd came back cringing as they heard the Alpha inside.

That night we all howled, together, for Stiles.

Chapter 3

I rubbed the sleep from my eyes letting out a yawn as I sat up. I looked around to see I was in a white room. Nothing in the room but the walls, a door, and the bed I was in. I looked down noticing I was in all white clothes too.

I got up and walked to the door. The cold floor stinging against my warm feet.

I pulled open the door to see another room, this time it was white with baby blue.

"Hello?" I called out, walking further into the room. It looked like a waiting room in a hospital.

"Oh Stiles!" I heard. I turned to see a women running toward me.

"M-Mom?" I asked as she wrapped her arms around me. "Is it really you?"

"Yes baby, it's me. Oh look how big you are." She smiled smushing my cheeks in her hands. "But, you're not supposed to be here." She said almost immediately.

"What do you mean? Where am I supposed to be?"

"With your pack silly." She laughed.

I rolled my eyes, "Yeah, okay."

"She's right kid." I turned to see my dad.

"Dad?" I felt my heart swell as he wrapped me in a hug.

"Hey kiddo." He said in my ear. "You have to go back."

I pulled away from him. "I-I don't want to."

"Honey, you have to. They need you." My mom said.

"No they don't! They'll be fine without me! I wanna stay here, with you." I felt tears sting my eyes.

"There's someone you need to meet." My dad lead me into another room.

"Stiles!" A women with long brown hair and a soft smile walked toward me. "Do you know who I am?"

"Talia...D-Derek's mom..." I said softly. I only ever saw Talia in pictures. I remember the first time Derek ever told me about her...

I picked up a photo that was sitting by Derek's bed. I smiled it was Derek and a women.

"Is this your mom?" I asked. He turned to look at me. "Uh, yeah. That's the last picture I got with her before the fire."

"You look just like her." I said softly, setting the photo down.

"Everyone used to say that." He chuckled lightly. "I'd give anything for two more minutes with her." He said tearing up. He quickly shook it off and straightened up, "come on, we have to go." He said rushing out of his room.

She nodded.

"He misses you." I said.

"And I him." She sighed, "but, Stiles honey, you can't stay here."

"Why?"

"Something big is coming. The pack is going to need you."

"I think they can handle it."

"How can I word this better for you..." She sat quietly for a moment. "There's a special kind of balance needed for a werewolf to be in sync with both his human side and his animal side."

"One zen werewolf required, great, I still don't get where I come in."

"Derek can't do this on his own, he needs you. You're his anchor."

I looked up at her in shock. "Me? But, no, that's not....his anger is his anchor..."

"Not anymore. Not only does Derek need you but the rest of the pack does too. You bring comfort, they will need that more than ever."

"They'll be fine. They're probably happy I'm gone. Especially Derek."

Talia sighed. "Why don't we show you."

The next thing I knew I was sitting outside the Hale House. Derek was sitting next to my body growling at anyone who came near.

"Derek, go inside!" Cora yelled. Derek sent out the loudest growl I've ever heard him muster.

I turned my attention to the front door that was just flung open.

"Scott!" Allison cried running after a very upset Scott.

"Leave me alone!" He yelled back, taking off into the woods.

I looked to see Erica, Boyd, and Jackson on the porch in silence. "We'll figure out who did this." The words floating out of Jackson's mouth were ice cold.

"Derek get up!" Cora cried, making me turn my attention back to the Alpha.

"Let me go, Cora!" He shouted, his voice cracking as he pushed her off of him.

"Derek!" She yelled, Derek finally breaking as he buried his face in his hands, Cora wrapping him in a hug immediately.

The twins walked out of the woods arguing about the guy who shot me. Lydia walked over to the house and wrapped Isaac in a hug who stood silently by himself.

"He can't be gone." He said, voice barely audible. "He can't be." A tear rolled down his face.

It got really quiet for a moment before I heard a howl. I turned toward Derek again to see him howling toward the sky. Cora joined in a second later. There was a howl in the distance that sounded like Scott. Isaac, the twins, Erica and Boyd, Jackson. Even the humans did their own little howl toward the sky.

"They need you Stiles." I heard my mom as the picture in front of me faded and we were placed back in the room from before.

"I need one thing..."

Chapter 4

I felt a pounding in my head. And I was cold, really cold. Someone's hand was in mine but my eyes were still too heavy to open. I noticed his hand was bigger than Scott's when I squeezed it.

"Derek." I said l, my voice rough.

"Stiles?"

"Derek, it's cold. Can we go inside?" I mumbled, feeling the grass under me.

"Oh my god! Stiles!" He yelled, pulling me into a hug.

"Come on big guy, get up. The rest of the pack needs to freak out too."

"Wait, how? You were..."

"I don't really know. Let me up." I said, pushing out of his grasp.

"W-wait. Get back here!" Derek yelled.

I laughed, "I'm right here." I said waiting for him to get off his ass.

Everyone got their hugs in and the heart attacks subsided.

"You got some explaining to do." Scott snapped.

"Honestly, I need food and a nap right now." I said, being pulled onto the couch by Derek.

"No, you need to explain."

"Scott, I don't know. I just, I woke up."

"You're seriously telling me that you have no idea how you magically came back to fucking life?"

"Sorry my presence is such a burden to you." I muttered to myself.

"Don't even do that right now." Scott said.

"What time is it?" I asked.

"Almost midnight." Isaac told me.

"Derek, Cora, I need you to come with me." I said, getting up.

"What the hell are you talking about?" Scott said. "You're not leaving."

I rolled my eyes and walked out of the house sitting on the hood of Derek's Camaro.

"Stiles what is going on?" I heard Derek seeing him and Cora.

"I just...we have to go. Please. You'll understand after."

"Stiles I'm not going anywhere, you just came back from the dead you don't need to be going anywhere."

"Derek we're running out of time. Please!" I begged.

"Come on Derek. What's the worst that could happen?" Cora asked, getting a glare.

"He could fucking die again?"

"Derek! Seriously! I'll explain everything to you but we need to go. Not only for me but for you!" I said.

"I swear to god." Derek groaned. "Fucking, ugh. Get in."

"Is it weird?" Cora asked.

"Is what weird?" I laughed, changing the radio station.

"Being alive again." She hit me.

"Honestly, it feels like I woke up with the flu." I said, settling on an alternative station.

"Then why the fuck aren't we at home!?" Derek snapped.

"Der, please. It'll make sense in a few minutes. Turn left." He sighed but turned.

"Stiles why the hell are we here?" Derek snapped as we pulled up to the cemetery.

"Because this is where I was told to go." I said getting out.

"Where the hell are you going?" He snapped following me.

"Derek just let him do what he has to do." Cora said following us.

"Guys. This way. Hurry." I said.

"Stiles, what are you doing?"

"Derek." I got right up next to him. "Please, just trust me. For once. Fucking trust me." I begged.

"Okay, okay. Go on." He said after a few moments.

"We've been sitting here for ten minutes." Derek grumbled to his sister.

"Stop being such an asshole. He just wanted to see his parents." She shot back.

"That's not want this is about." I said softly. "Just, wait a few more minutes. Please." I said feeling my chest tighten.

Please tell me I didn't miss them. Please tell me it was real. This is the only reason I agreed to come back.

"Stiles." Derek said softly, touching my arm.

"J-just a few minutes. Please." I begged, starting to cry.

There was dead silence for a solid five minutes before I heard it.

"Derek, Cora...?" I turned around to see Derek staring at me.

"Mom?" I heard Cora cry.

"Derek." It was a man's voice.

I watched Derek turn around.

"Mom, Dad?" His voice was shaky.

"Wow, leave your favorite sister out." Laura laughed.

I sat next to my mom's grave watching, for the first time ever I saw Derek crying and smiling and truly happy.

I walked back to the car waiting, knowing that this wouldn't last much longer. I sat in the passenger seat sending Scott a text to let him know we would be home soon. I looked up to see Derek and Cora walking back. Derek had his arm wrapped around his younger sister and she was wrapped around him. We drove home was silence. I watched Derek wipe his face several times and Cora sniffled in the back seat. When we pulled into the driveway she pressed a kiss to my cheek as a silent 'Thank you' and walked inside.

"How'd you do that?" Derek stopped me before I got inside.

I wasn't sure how to explain everything. I didn't even understand it all.

"You know what, I don't care." He said. "Thank you."

I nodded giving him a hug. I felt him hug back, "Seriously, thank you so much." He said into my neck.

"You're welcome, Der."

Chapter 5

"Derek?" Stiles called, walking into the Alpha's room.

"Yeah?" Derek replied, pulling a shirt on.

"Can you take me to Deaton's?"

"Why?" He asked.

"Because I need to talk to him." Stiles replied sitting on the unmade bed.

"Ask Scott." Derek finally turned to face the other.

"I don't want Scott, I want you." Stiles said in the most serious voice he could.

"Why?"

"Because you're alpha. And I think you should be there with me."

"Are you scared of something?" Derek asked. "Because Scott can protect yo-"

"That's not what this is about, Derek." Stiles whined. "I just want you to take me. Please?"

Derek sighed, "Can it be after my run?" He asked almost whining.

Stiles nodded falling back onto the bed.

"Are you okay?" Derek asked.

"I'm tired."

Derek nodded, "Okay...I'm gonna..."

"Yeah, you do that." Stiles yawned, curling himself into Derek's pillow.

Stiles POV

I listened to Derek walk around his room for a few minutes before chuckling to himself and walking toward me. I've been so tired since I came back from the dead. That's what the pack keeps calling it. I mean its true but they're all dramatic about it. Part of me wishes I was still dead. It's not like I'm doing anything special. I felt him pull his blanket over top of me. He stood there letting out a sigh before walking out of his room. I was being washed away as sleep overcame me. I breathed in Derek's scent. Pine, fire, and nutmeg. He smelled like home.

I woke to the sound of Derek's bathroom door shutting. I yawned rubbing my eyes. I had the weirdest dream. Flashes. One second it was of Derek. Then Scott. Then Lydia. It continued throughout the whole pack. I remember this one flash, specifically because it was horrifying.

The pack was gone. And I don't mean they went for a walk. I mean someone or something came in and killed them. I remember I woke up sitting in between Derek and Scott, their blood pooling around me, soaking my clothes. Thinking about it gives me chills.

I heard the shower turn off. After a few minutes Derek walked out in his boxers rubbing a towel against his head.

"You're up." He said, almost happily. I nodded in reply watching him stalk over to his closet and pull out another set of clothes to put on.

"Do you feel better?" He asked.

I shook my head trying to pull the blanket closer. "Worse." I said, my voice cracking before I broke out into a coughing fit.

Derek frowned, "Come on, lets get you to Deaton's. Maybe he'll know how to make you feel better."

"Okay." I said not moving.

"You have to actually get up you know." Derek joked.

"I'm cold."

Derek pulled me out of his bed grabbing his leather jacket from the end and handing it to me. "Come on."

Chapter 6

Derek POV

We drove to Deaton's in complete silence. Stiles had his head against the window with his eyes closed. He looked exhausted. I pulled into the parking lot getting out and helping a half asleep Stiles from the car. He leaned into me as we walked inside.

"You're so much warmer than your jacket." He muttered, pushing his face into my neck. I laughed waiting for Deaton to finish whatever it was he was doing.

"So, boys. What can I help you with?"

"Can you make sure Stiles is okay?" I asked feeling the boy push off of me.

"I know I'm not okay. I feel like I'm dying. It's so warm in here. Oh my god." He said pulling off my jacket.

"Derek, you do know I'm a vet right?" Deaton asked.

"Yes. I know. But Stiles died and came back to life so I can't really take him to an actual doctor."

Deaton hummed, telling Stiles to get onto the metal table.

"So, you died?" He started. "Explain that to me."

"I pushed Derek out of the way and I got hit instead." Stiles said.

"He wasn't even near me. No one in the pack even knew someone was there." I added.

Stiles rolled his eyes. "I don't know how. He was so obvious."

"Do you remember anything when you were...dead..?" Deaton asked cutting off our small conversation.

"I saw my parents." Stiles smiled, sadly. "And I met Derek's mom. She told me I had to come back." He looked at me. "I didn't want to come back."

"But you did?" Deaton asked.

"I said I'd come back for the pack if they did one thing for me. They followed through on their end so...here I am."

"What are you talking about?" I cut Deaton off.

"I came back for you. So...so you could see your parents and sister one last time. You deserved it...so I came back even though I didn't want to." He said quietly.

"Are you crazy? Stiles, you could've had anything!"

Stiles let out a small laugh. "Der, I saw you truly happy for the first time. I got what I wanted."

"What about your parents?" Deaton cut me off again.

"I see them. I don't know if it's real...but when I sleep I'm back there again. I get to see all of my family. My grandma and grandpa. My dad. My mom. My aunt that passed away when I was little. Everyone." He paused. "The pain stops when I'm with them."

Deaton leaned against the wall. Probably trying to figure out what was wrong with Stiles.

"Der...can I have your jacket back?" Stiles broke the silence. I nodded handing it back.

"Do you feel sick?" Deaton asked.

Stiles nodded. "I feel like I have the flu or something. I didn't think it was a big deal. Which reminds me...I uh...probably should've showed you this when we got here. I forgot." He said setting my jacket next to him and pulling his shirt off.

He sighed and squeezed his eyes shut. A second later I was hit. By a wing. A white fucking wing.

"Oh. Yes. You should have started with that." Deaton said. "Can you change your eyes?" He asked.

Stiles blinked, his eyes changing to a red color. Deaton nodded looking unsatisfied.

I touched his wing making him move it away. "Don't. It tickles." He said softly changing his eyes back and retracting his wings.

Deaton handed Stiles a book. "Read this, it will help you. The sick feeling will pass in a week or so."

"This is a book about angels? Are you saying I'm an angel?" Stiles asked.

"I believe so. A guardian to be specific. The book will explain everything. Just get some rest and read."

Stiles nodded jumping off of the counter and walked out toward the car.

"Derek." Deaton stopped me. "Watch him. He's in pain."

"How do you know?" I asked.

"His eyes are red. They should be lilac. Unlike wolves there aren't alphas. Some angels are stronger but they don't need a pack for safety. The eyes tend to reflect mood. Lilac is natural. They are happy, content. Red means pain both physically and mentally. Blue is mental pain, sadness. Orange is anger. Yellow, physical pain alone. Pink means he's nervous. That normally happens only when with someone they love."

He sighed continuing. "I want you to read that book too. He needs you right now. The way he felt before he died is the way he feels now. He needs to know that the pack appreciates him, especially after he helps you guys battle. If he feels unwanted, he'll stop saving you. He'll hurt himself. It's explained in the book. Read it."

Chapter 7

D erek POV

    I followed Stiles inside. Isaac was sitting on the couch and gave us a small wave as we walked inside.

"Where'd you guys go?" He asked.

Stiles walked up the stairs still wearing my jacket, his arms cradling the book Deaton gave him.

"To see Deaton." I said.

"Anything interesting?"

"Maybe." I said walking upstairs.

I walked into my room to see Stiles curled up in my bed. The book was sitting on my desk.

"You okay?" I asked, walking over to sit by him.

He shook his head. "I don't feel good."

"Do you want anything?"

"I want to feel better." He said.

I rolled my eyes hearing him laugh before coughing. "I'm serious."

He sighed, "Can you just lay with me?" His voice was low and I almost wasn't sure I heard him. "You don't have to." He added.

"It's fine." I said, laying down next to him. "Come here, angel."

He laughed, "Shut up."

Scott POV

I got over to Derek's for the pack meeting to find everyone except Derek and Stiles.

"They went upstairs and haven't come down." Isaac said, answering the confused expression on my face.

"Oh..." I started. "Why didn't anyone go get them?"

"We were gonna but they're sleeping." Lydia said.

"And neither of them have been sleeping great lately." Isaac cut in again.

"And..." Lydia glared at Isaac. "They're cuddling and it's just too cute to break up."

"Stiles and Derek?" I asked. "Huh, okay." I said going upstairs.

I heard Stiles and Derek talking softly to each other as I made my way to his room.

"I'm sorry I didn't tell you." I heard Stiles.

"You told me today." Derek replied.

"I know but I feel like I should've said something when it happened."

I heard Derek sigh, "It's honestly not a big deal. Do you want the pack to know?"

"I dunno. Maybe after we know for sure."

"Okay."

I waited a minute before walking into his doorway and knocking.

"Yeah?" Derek asked not bothering to look up at me. Stiles was laying on his chest and he was rubbing the others back.

"Everyone's here..." I said.

"Okay. I'll be down in a few minutes."

I nodded watching them for a few more moments before walking downstairs.

Stiles POV

I sat up so Derek could get out of bed. I watched him walk to his closet and change from his jeans to sweatpants.

"Thanks." He turned to face me giving me a confused look.

"For?" He asked.

I sat quietly for a minute, "Cuddling with me." I said quietly.

He nodded, "Come on." I sighed seeing him hold out a hand to pull me off the bed.

"Wait." I stopped him from pulling me downstairs. "I know you're a were-wolf and stuff...but do you have anything for my headache?"

He bit the inside of his cheek and looked around aimlessly for a minute before raising his eyebrows and walking into the bathroom connected to his room.

He brought a pill bottle out to me. "Here."

"Thanks."

"Yeah, c'mon." He said wrapping an arm around me.

I sat through the meeting not focusing on what was being discussed. Derek didn't push the subject of me "being an angel" which I still think is crazy, but I was thankful. I feel like I haven't slept in weeks. My head is pounding. I'm nauseous. I'm honestly just falling apart.

Scott pulled me aside after the meeting. He sat there staring at me. Not saying a word, just staring.

"What?" I laughed.

"Is there something going on?" He started. "Between you and Derek?"

"No, why?"

"You guys were cuddling, Stiles."

I laughed, "He was just trying to help me feel better. He'd do it to anyone else in the pack too, you know that."

"You know, you can tell me anything right?"

"Yes Scott, that's normally how our friendship works." I sighed.

"I just...don't want you to think I'm gonna hate you or something...if you know...there is something going on."

"Scott, I promise you, there isn't anything going on. He was trying to make me feel better."

Scott nodded, "Did you go see Deaton?"

"Yeah, we're not totally sure what's wrong." I lied, hoping Scott either doesn't notice or ignored it.

"I'm sure he'll figure it out. Try to feel better." He smiled.

I nodded following him into the kitchen. Isaac smiled at us as we walked in, Scott immediately going over to the other.

"What are you making?" I asked, walking over to Derek who was at the stove.

"Soup." He replied.

I laughed, leaning closer to him. "Scott thinks we're fucking." I whispered to him.

He turned to look at Scott and Isaac before turning back to me. "Would that be so bad?" He whispered in my ear biting on the top before walking away.

Excuse me, what just happened?

Chapter 8

D erek POV

"D-Derek!" I heard Stiles call from the living room.

I walked down the hall hearing him whine and what seemed to be him stomping his foot on the ground. I got into the living room to see his wings spread from one end of the room to the other.

"What are you doing?" I asked. "The packs on their way back?"

"I didn't do it! I can't get them to go back!" He said, worry lacing his words. "Derek, I don't want them to find out. Not like this!"

"Relax. You remember how we train new betas? What do they use to help them during the full moon?"

"Alpha, beta, omega. But, I don't have that!"

"The sun, the moon, the truth." I said.

"It's not going to work!" He yelled.

"Stiles, trust me."

He whined beginning to whisper to himself. "It's not working!" He said his eyes beginning to flash between various colors.

"Find an anchor."

"I don't know how!" He yelled.

"Think of someone. Let them keep you grounded. Just think of them."

"I thought you weren't supposed to use people as an anchor?" He asked.

"Just do it." I growled.

"Don't growl at me." He rubbed his hands over his face.

"Come on, Stiles. You can do this."

I watched his eyes drop shut and a small smile cover his face. A few more moments passed before his wings were gone and he was looking at me again.

"Thanks." He said softly his eyes flashing a shade of pink before going back to brown. I smiled and nodded.

(A/N: the picture is what his eye color is supposed to look like. That and it's pretty.)

"Derek." Stiles barged into my room.

"Yes?" I asked, turning around.

"Help me fly."

"Help you fly? Yes, because I know how to work wings."

"Come on! The packs gone, you train them, you help them, how much different can it be?"

"Extremely?" I laughed, "Stiles, I have no clue how to help you."

"You're just not up for a challenge."

I shook my head, "Why don't we finish reading and then talk about flying?"

"I don't want to read anymore. I'm always reading."

"Then let me finish reading."

"Fine. But, I'm taking a nap while you read. Right here." He said, climbing into my bed and curling the blankets around him.

I grabbed the book and sat down next to him. I felt him curl closer to me. I wrapped an arm around him, sighed, and opened the book.

Some angels are known to develop powers.

Like most supernatural creatures the senses are heightened; taste, smell, sight, hearing, touch.

Some of the known and most common powers found in angels are;

-mind reading-increased intelligence in various fields-super speed-capability of predicting the future-communication with animals-mimicing others voices-invisibility-can breath underwater-can heal others by mind and/or touch-can kill someone by touch if they choose

Various types of angels can do different things.

AngelsAren't a harm to anyone. Only provides help. They tend to be the kindest of all angels.

ReapersThese angels serve death. They are demonic creatures that feed off pain and sorrow. Use possession to control others into getting what they desire.

Fallen AngelAngels who have lost their powers. Fallen angels tend to fall into the path of a Reaper.

GuardiansGuardians are created for the sole purpose of protection. When one cares more for others than themselves is when the Guardian is awakened. They are very emotional beings and need to be taken care of just as much as they care for others.

Angelic Tendencies:

Dream Walking:Angels can appear in people's dreams, they usually use this to communicate, when they can't find the person they're looking for, or want to talk privately.

Electronic Manipulation:Angelic beings tend to be able to manipulate electronics.

Regeneration:Like most supernatural beings, angels can heal at extreme rates.

Sedation:More common in Reapers, angels can cause humans to fall unconscious with a touch.

"Derek, stop reading." Stiles' voice broke my attention from the book as he wrapped himself around my leg. "Someone's here." He yawned.

"It's Scott." I said. He nodded.

I heard Scott walk inside and up the stairs toward my room. He stood in the doorway out of breath.

"We have a problem."

This is more informational than anything. Sorry.

Merry Christmas!!!!!!

Chapter 9

"We have a problem." Scott said.

"What exactly do you mean?"

"There's some lady outside. She's like super pissed and wants to see you like right now."

"Fuck." I groaned, pushing Stiles from my leg and getting up. I heard the two follow me downstairs and outside.

"Derek. I wish I could say it's good to see you." She smiled.

"What did Peter do now, Edith?" I sighed.

"He killed my sister. So, now. I'm going to kill you." She smiled.

"Excuse me?" I heard Stiles.

"Stiles." I snapped.

"Why don't you just kill Peter?" Stiles continued. "Derek didn't do any-thing?"

"And how would you know?" She took her attention off me and locked it on him.

"Because...I just do.." he looked up at me.

I sighed, "Go back inside, Stiles." He whined next to me.

"That's so cute." She laughed harshly. "Although, I have no idea where Peter is and I'm sure Derek would rather die over me killing his poor baby sister."

Cora growled from the porch. "Leave him alone, bitch!"

"CORA!" I yelled.

"No!" I heard Stiles.

Stiles POV

I heard Derek yell at his sister. As he turned around the witch got this angry look and the next thing I knew I was by Derek's side with my wings wrapped around both of us. I whimpered into Derek's chest as I felt a burning sensation on my wing and the witch start laughing.

"Huh, I didn't know you had a Guardian, Derek. Why didn't you tell me?"

"Its not really on my list of priorities." He snarled wrapping his arm around my waist to drain some pain.

She hummed to herself. "Let me help you with that." She walked closer touching my wing. I moved it hearing Derek growl at her. "I'm just trying to help. He wasn't meant to get hurt, you were." She said, moving her fingers toward me mumbling some words. Derek growled pushing me behind him.

"Too late." She whispered before dissapearing.

"D-Derek." I mumbled gripping onto his arm.

"You okay? Stiles?"

I looked at him before everything darkened. I rubbed my eyes opening them and seeing nothing again.

"Stiles, what's wrong?" I could hear the pack getting closer.

"I can't see." I said my grip getting tighter. "I can't see."

"What do you mean you can't see?" I heard Scott.

"I mean I can't see!" I yelled.

"We have to go to Deaton. Put your wings away." Derek said.

"It still hurts." I said stumbling feeling Derek help me.

"Is someone going to explain the wings?" Jackson asked.

"Not now." Derek snapped. "Come on, Stiles."

"What did Deaton say?" I heard, Isaac as Derek helped me inside.

"He thinks he has something that will help but he won't be able to get it until tomorrow." Derek said.

"Can you explain the wings now?" Scott said.

Derek led me to the couch sitting next to me. "Do I have to?" I asked.

"Kinda?" Scott said.

I rubbed my face and sighed. I started explaining everything to them. I was trying to focus on what I could hear and feel rather than trying to see. I knew it was just a spell, I knew it would wear off. But, I was still scared.

I felt a hand on my back as Derek spoke softly into my ear. "I'm gonna go read some more. Do you want to come up with me?" He asked.

I heard Scott and Isaac talking about some video game and the TV turn on as the rest of the pack found something to busy themselves with. "Yeah." I sighed.

"Derek..." I sighed laying on his bed.

"Yeah?" I heard him turn a page in the book.

"I have to pee." I said, quietly feeling my face heat up.

I heard him chuckle and get up. "Come on." He grabbed my hand as he got to the other side of the bed.

"Thanks." I mumbled as he led me to his bathroom.

"I hope you know I'm not helping with the rest of that."

I laughed, "Didn't want you too, big guy."

--

"Derek!"

"Stiles, I already told you I-"

"No, I wanted you to help me to my room. Please? I want to take a nap."

"Oh. Okay." I heard the shuffle of his feet and his grip around my arm.

"Sorry I can't see..."

"Don't apologize. You were protecting me. So what, you pissed off a witch and now you're temporarily blind. It's not a big deal."

After I was set on my bed Derek spoke up again. "Just, uh...call me if you need anything."

"Are you still reading the book from Deaton?"

"Yeah."

I nodded, "Thanks." I laid down hearing him walk out.

"See, Stiles. They need you around." I heard. I turned to come face to face with Derek's older sister, Laura.

"I don't think me pissing off a witch and not being able to see is any help toward them."

"You protected my brother. Just like you would if it was Scott or Isaac or anyone else in the pack."

"Y-yeah, but that doesn't mean anything."

She sighed "God, I really want to punch you."

I snorted. 'Yep, Derek's sister.' I thought.

"You'll understand more after you get control over this."

I sighed. "So, is this like a weird dream or something?"

"Kinda." She said, sitting down cross legged on the white floor.

"Are you real or like...just a dream?"

"I'm real. Or at least as real as a dead girl can be." I gave her a confused look getting an eye roll in return. "Look, instead of having dreams when you sleep, you get to hang here. With me, my family, your family, basically anyone who's dead."

"Where is 'here' exactly?" I asked.

"We like to call it Serenity." She sighed. "It's kind of a meeting place between the dead world-mine-and the living world-yours-for people like you to meet up with people like me. It's another cool privilege angels get."

"Oh..." I said softly.

"You can wander into people's dreams too. Its called Dream Walking. Go mess with Derek sometime. It'd be hilarious. You have to tell me all about it. Get him all flustered for me." She laughed.

"Wait, I can really do that? How?"

She shrugged. "I'm not an angel. I'm guessing it's just a skill you develop over time, ya know?"

I nodded, feeling as if I was being pulled from wherever I was.

"I'll see you later, Stiles." She smiled.

I yawned rubbing my eyes panicking slightly before I remembered I couldn't see anything.

"You okay, bro?" I heard Scott.

"Y-yeah. I'm good, Scotty."

"Okay. If you need anything I'll be in my room. Just call." He said. I could picture the goofy smile on his face.

I slowly got up off my bed finding my way to my door. I tried picturing the layout of the upstairs to find my way back to Derek's room. I knocked on a door not sure if I had the right room. I sighed hearing a small groan followed by a "yeah?"

I opened the door and heard Derek making his way over to me. "Tell me about Dream Walking."

Chapter 10

"Tell me about Dream Walking." Stiles blurted.

"I don't really know much about it."

"Then tell me what you do know."

I sighed, "I know that you can go into people's dreams and talk to them. That's about it. I don't know how to do it, I don't know if the other person you talk to will remember it or think it's just a dream, I don't know, Stiles."

He frowned, "but you're reading that book..."

"It doesn't say much. The book wasn't written by an angel. I'm sorry but you're going to have to figure some of this stuff out on your own."

He sighed, leaning against the door frame. "It saw Laura." He whispered. "She told me she wanted to punch me." He chuckled.

"Sounds like Laura." I smiled.

He sighed, "I wish I could bring them back for you."

"You did." I said getting up.

"I mean...for good."

"You've done more than enough for me, Stiles." He sighed, "You know, Stiles." I started, my hand wrapping gently around his neck, "There's actually still one thing you haven't done for me."

"What's that?"

"You haven't ever made me a sandwich."

Stiles snorted, letting out a loud laugh. "I'll make you sandwich when I can see again."

"I'm holding you to that."

"Stiles, get up." I said shaking him.

"No." He groaned, rolling into his pillow.

"Stiles." I growled.

He sighed, "What?"

"Open your eyes."

"No?"

"Do it."

He opened his eyes. "Why? I can't see anything."

"Deaton dropped off these eye drops this morning. They'll bring back your sight."

"How long will it take?"

"He said it could start working at anytime but I have to do it every four hours until you can see again."

"Is it going to take days?"

"It could. No more than 3 I think he said."

Stiles nodded. "Okay, do it."

He flinched a little as the drop touched his eyes right before they started watering.

"Ow, what the hell is in that?"

"I don't know." I chuckled as he sat up. "Come on, breakfast is downstairs."

He nodded, pushing himself off his bed. I grabbed his upper arm before he tried walking downstairs by himself.

"Ow, Derek, claws." He said hitting me. I hadn't even noticed. "What the hell?" He asked as I retracted my claws.

"I-I don't know, I'm sorry, I didn't..."

"Whatever, It's fine." He said grabbing my sleeve with his other hand.

I laid in my bed, falling backwards. Stiles' scent filled the air as I hit the pillow. I keep forgetting how much time he's spent in here lately. I keep forgetting that I don't seem to mind. I bit my lip feeling it split open and the taste of metallic fill my mouth.

"What the hell?" I asked myself bringing my hand up to my mouth feeling my canines showing. I rolled my eyes sighing. "I'm losing it." I groaned rolling onto my stomach and burying my face into the pillow.

I sniffed in more of Stiles' scent feeling a growl rise up my through and my claws poke through the pillowcase. "Ugh." I rubbed my hands over my face.

"Derek!" my door swung open and I felt an extra 147 pounds on top of me. "I can see again! That stuff worked!" Stiles yelled, hugging me. I hugged him back feeling my wolf settle and my claws retract themselves. "What'd you do?" He asked, sitting up to look at me.

"What're you..?"

"Your lip." He said poking my lip. "It's bleeding."

"I bit it." I said staring at him. He nodded. "I'm gonna go play video games with Scott. I'm having withdrawals." He laughed getting up. "Thanks for helping me, Der."

I sighed, watching him walk out.

I walked into the kitchen around eleven that night to find Stiles standing at the counter reading the back of a box.

"What're you doing?" I asked.

"Figuring out how long to cook these." He said gesturing to the pan full of brownie mix behind him.

"You're making brownies? This late?" I laughed.

He nodded, "They sounded good."

I watched him smile as he found the right time to keep them in the oven and started the timer. He started washing the dishes when I clenched my jaw feeling my wolf fighting against me.

"Can I talk to you?" He asked not looking at me.

"Yup." I grunted squeezing my eyes shut.

"How do you do it?"

"Do what?"

"Be fine all the time. You're family burned in a fire and you're perfectly fine. How are you fine!? Because I'm not close to fine. All I could think about when I couldn't see was my mom and my dad and how much it fucking hurts. I don't understand."

"I'm not fine." I sighed, pulling him away from the sink. "I'm not close to fine it just...got easier."

"But it hurts so much."

"I know." I watched him dry his hands.

"It's so stupid. I can see them. I have seen them. B-But it still hurts. Why's it still hurt?"

"Seeing them in whatever dream world you get to see them in, isn't the same as seeing them. As having them here with you."

He wiped his face looking up at me. "What's wrong?" He asked.

"What're you talking about?"

"Your eyes are red."

"I-I'm fine. It's nothing. Probably the full moon coming up." I said shaking my head.

He nodded. "Okay.." he hugged me.

I wrapped my arms around him feeling my wolf finally start to calm down.

What the actual fuck is happening?

Chapter 11

D erek POV

"Hey," I said, walking toward Stiles who was sitting on the couch. He tore his gaze from his laptop to look up at me. "I'm going to the store. Do you need anything?"

"Uh...I don't think so, but thanks." He said with a smile.

I nodded walking out and making my way to the store. That's when it happened.

I walked passed an aisle full of stuffed animals, specifically, teddy bears. I wasn't surprised because Valentine's Day is coming up but something made me stop and pick one up. It looked familiar and I couldn't figure out why. As soon as I picked it up a sharp pain shot through my body making my head pound.

"Derek." The small boy next to me wouldn't shut up. "Derek!" He whined. "Don't be sad!" He frowned. "My daddy said he's gonna help. He's gonna make it better." He started kicking his feet that were hanging off the bench in the hospital.

I rubbed my eyes. "What the fuck." I muttered dropping the bear trying to continue through the store. The pain came back, worse than before.

"You wanna meet my momma!?" The kid said happily. "Come on! She's super nice!" He said jumping off the bench and pulling me up. He dragged me toward one of the hospital rooms and climbed onto the bed next to who I assume is his mom. "Mom! Look! This is Derek!" He said happily. I forced a smile toward her as she greeted me. "Stiles," I turned to see the Sheriff behind me. "Your mother needs to rest, you need to let her. I told you that." He sighed. "I just wanted Derek to meet her." Stiles frowned. His mother hugged him. "And I did, now go, run along." She said softly. "It was nice meeting you, Derek." She smiled toward me. "You too." I said softly.

I groaned holding onto my head. I abandoned the cart full of groceries and made my way back to my car. "Stop." I said resting my head on the steering wheel right before I felt my head explode again.

"Dad!" I sat back on the bench while Stiles followed his dad around the waiting room. "Dad!" He called again. "What, Stiles?" His dad sighed. "Can I have ten dollars?" He asked smiling up at the Sheriff. "Why?" His dad asked. "Just...please! I wanna get something!" He begged. "You need to find somewhere to sit down." His father said sternly. The pale boy groaned "I gotta do something first!" The sheriff sighed handing him a ten dollar bill. "You go sit somewhere. Got it?" Stiles nodded happily before he ran into the little gift shop they had full of flowers and cards and other 'get well soon' gifts. He ran over to me with a small light brown teddy bear. "Here." He smiled. "Why?" I asked. "Because you're sad. And even though you're a big kid...sometimes it helps to hug a teddy bear." He smiled jumping back onto the bench next to me. "Thanks." I sighed seeing him smile.

I walked inside to see the pack gathered by Stiles in the living room. I groaned leaning against the back of the door. I felt my fangs scraping my teeth.

"Derek?" I heard Stiles' voice. It sounded like we were miles apart. The room was spinning. I felt a growl rise up my throat as I climbed up the stairs. Flashes of the fire invading my vision. "Derek!?" Stiles said again. I could hear the pack following me.

"Derek!" I looked up seeing Stiles in front of me. I was in the Sheriff's office at the station now. "Derek, wake up!" He laughed. "My dad got us pizza!" He said trying to pull me off the couch. "I'm not hungry." I groaned. "Derek!" He whined.

"...Derek!" I saw Stiles sitting in front of me in my room. I yelled in pain pushing Stiles as lightly as I could back toward the pack.

Stiles POV

"Hey," I heard Derek. I looked away from my laptop to see him standing above me by the couch. "I'm going to the store. Do you need anything?" He asked.

"Uh...I don't think so, but thanks." I said back to him. He nodded before he left. Shortly after, the pack came over to me.

"So, you and Derek?" Scott smirked.

"What about me and Derek?"

"You didn't tell us you guys are a thing?" Lydia smiled.

"That's because we're not?"

Isaac burst into laughter, "Oh my god, you can't be serious right now?"

I rolled my eyes focusing back on my laptop, "We're not...are we?" I glanced up at Scott.

"You totally are. How are you this oblivious?" He answered.

"I just...we haven't...he only helps me with this whole angel thing."

"Stiles, honey, you guys are totally a thing. You sleep in the same bed more than Jackson and I do." Lydia said.

I heard the front door slam shut and turned to see Derek wolfed out. "Derek?" I called watching him stumble up the stairs. "Derek!?" I tried again. I watched him fall onto his floor pushing himself against his bed. His red eyes were glazed over and you could tell he was in pain. "Derek!" I tried once more seeing him finally come back. He yelled his screams mixing with a roar right before he pushed me back toward the pack. Scott pulled me up close to him. I felt a pain in my chest as Derek curled into himself on the floor screaming again. Soon his screams subsided and I felt the urge to go comfort him. Scott pulled me back. "Derek?" I said softly.

"You." He said softly, out of breathe. "I-I knew you."

"What are you talking about?" I asked looking up at Scott.

Derek pushed himself off the floor and stumbled to his closet. He handed me a stuffed bear. "I knew you."

I looked down at the bear and smiled. "You still have it." He squeezed his eyes shut in pain.

"What is that? What are you guys talking about?" Isaac asked.

"He gave me that the night my family died." Derek said softly climbing into his bed. "And forced me to meet his mom."

"I made you eat pizza too." I smiled sadly.

"Did you even know what was going on?" He asked.

I shook my head, "But you were upset and alone in the hospital with my dad." I watched his hands go up to his head. "I forgot about this."

"Yeah, I did too. Until I just relived it." He groaned.

I looked at the pack before climbing in bed cuddling up next to Derek. "Now you can hug me and the bear." I said making him snort as he wrapped an arm around me.

"Shut up, Stiles." He smirked tiredly.

The rest of the pack started climbing into the bed with us to help Derek feel better. I smiled curling into Derek more as he slowly drifted off. I watched Isaac glue himself to Derek's other side. He sent a small smile toward me before I myself let sleep consume me.

Derek POV

I woke up only feeling the weight of one person on me. My headache was gone but I still felt like I had been hit by a bus. I needed to go see Deaton. I looked down at Stiles who was now completely on top of me, his head buried in the crook of my neck. I smiled wrapping my arms tighter around him making him let out a quiet sigh. He kissed my neck before nuzzling into me.

"Der..." he groaned. I rubbed his back feeling him shift his position on me. "Please..." He moaned. I chuckled at him. He was still asleep and it was adorable. He let out another small Moana "Alright." I said to myself before shaking him awake.

"What?" He groaned, rubbing his eyes.

"You know you talk in your sleep, right?" I asked making him blush.

He pushed himself off of me, "I'm sorry." He whispered. I pulled him closer to me as I sat up pressing a kiss right under his ear.

"I gotta go see Deaton." I told him. He nodded his face brighter red now than it was a few seconds ago. I pushed myself out of bed seeing the small bear fall to the floor as I stood up. I picked it up setting it back on my bed before I walked out of my room.

"Fuck." I heard Stiles groan and what sounded like him falling back onto my bed.

I smiled to myself before making my way to Deaton's. I explained how my wolf has been acting up and how I painfully relived the worst day of my life and the day I actually met Stiles without even knowing it. Deaton gave me a soft smile.

"Well, it sounds to me like you've found your mate." He said happily.

"My what?"

Chapter 12

"Derek!" I called watching him walk into the kitchen. "Derek, are you gonna help me today?"

"Can't." He grunted walking past me toward the front door.

"Why not?"

"I have to go." I watched him pull on his jacket and grab his keys.

"Where?"

"We need milk."

"There's 3 gallons in the fridge?" I questioned.

Derek growled, "We. Need. Milk." He said, storming out of the house.

He came home 5 hours later without milk.

This started becoming a normal thing. Derek returned to his normal closed off self. He wasn't talking anymore. He wouldn't even look at me. I don't know what I did wrong. Maybe he just wants me to leave. Find my own place. But, we were getting so close, we were a thing. We totally are a thing. So, what happened?

I sighed hearing the front door shut again and Derek drive off in his Camaro. It's late, close to 2 in the morning. I pushed myself from my bed and climbed into his. Maybe if I stay here long enough he'll finally have no choice but to talk to me again.

"Hey, shithead." I heard Laura laugh.

I rolled my eyes sitting down next to her, "Do you know what Derek's problem is?"

"Derek's problem?" She asked. "You mean other than being a big bag of emotional constipation? No."

"He's being weird. I don't know what to do."

"Talk to him."

"He won't let me."

We sat in silence, comfortable silence. I wasn't expecting anyone else to show up tonight. But, I was wrong. I saw Derek's mom, Talia, and both of my parents.

"Hey, kiddo." My mom called sitting by me. I leaned into her.

"Hi, mom."

"Stiles, honey, could I talk to you alone for just a moment?" Talia asked. I looked over at Laura who shrugged before I stood up and followed Talia. The room around us changed from its normal cloudy white to a light blue and she stood quietly before speaking up.

"I need you to listen closely..."

Derek POV

I've been ignoring Stiles for the past few weeks and I know it's hurting him but I don't know what else to do. He's my mate. My mate. How am I supposed to tell him that? What am I even supposed to do? I spent most of my days just driving around so I didn't have to see him. I just don't want to mess anything up. I always mess something up. I try so, so hard, and it's never enough. I want to finally get something right...

I sat down feeling the dew on the grass cover my pants. I sighed resting my face into my hands. "I don't know what to do." I said softly. I pushed the leaves that had fallen onto the gravestone off. "I just wish you were here to tell me what to do." I felt my chest tighten and a tear fall down my face. "Please, just tell me what to do. I don't want to mess it up." I wiped off my face. "I just really need you right now, mom."

I don't know how long I sat there but when I finally got up to leave the sun had already rose and was beginning to set again. The drive home was a blur. Walking up the stairs was a blur. Walking into my room was a blur. Noticing Stiles sleeping in my bed was clear as day. I changed out of my pants and climbed into my bed next to him. I wrapped my arms around him and pulled him closer to me. He turned in my arms mumbling as his eyes fluttered open.

"Der?" He smiled bringing his hand up to rest on my cheek.

"Go back to sleep." I said softly.

He hummed, closing his eyes and curling into me more. "Your mom said to relax. She said you know what you need to do and to stop fighting it, bun bun." He said softly. "Whatever that means."

I snorted letting sleep overcome me just barely hearing Stiles ask "Does she call you 'bun bun' because you have cute little bunny teeth?"

Chapter 13

Mom's right. Mom's always right. Of course I know what to do. Well. Kind of. I just have to figure out how to do it.

Foods always a good choice. I could get a deer.

No, this is Stiles. If I bring him a deer that I killed...he'll kill me.

I'll just take him out to get curly fries. Yeah. That's good. He'll like that.

--

"Derek!" I heard as I got out of my car. I looked up to see Stiles standing on the roof.

"What the hell are you doing!?" I yelled back.

"Watch!" He smiled stepping back a bit before hurling himself off the roof. His wings spread out and he was flying. He figured it out. He taught himself how to fly.

I watched him lowered himself back down to the ground and retract his wings. "It's awesome isn't it!?"

I nodded, "Good job, Stiles." He smiled. "You wanna go get something to eat?"

"The answer to that question will always be yes." He replied.

--

I listened to Stiles ramble on about his college classes while we ate. The smile on his face seemed to melt everything else going on around us.

"Oh!" He started, "Here." He pulled out his wallet.

"It's on me." I said.

With a sigh he asked, "Are you sure?" I nodded. "Well..then...can I get another milkshake?"

I laughed, "You can get whatever you want."

He squealed thanking me as he gulped down the last little bit of his current milkshake.

--

Stiles POV

I got home early on Monday because my professor cancelled class, which thank God because I just really didn't want to go today. Unfortunately, nobody was home when I got there.

I sighed as the doorbell rang in the middle of my Supernatural marathon. I set the book Deaton told me to read about angels to the side as I got up. It's totally for show in case someone walks in I can pretend like I'm not wasting my life away. I answered the door seeing a delivery guy with a bouquet of flowers.

"Uh, hi?" I said.

"I have a delivery for a Stiles Stilinski?"

"That'd be me." I said taking them from him, "Thanks."

He grunted before walking away. I closed the door setting them on the kitchen counter. There isn't a card or anything with it. I wonder who they're from? Scott's probably just being a douche. Who knows.

--

"Hey." I jumped seeing Derek behind me.

"Hi, when'd you get home?"

"Like two seconds ago." He said opening the fridge. "Flowers?"

"Yeah, someone sent them but I don't know who." I watched him open a bottle of water and lean against the counter as he took a drink. "It's probably some kind of joke."

Derek set the bottle on the counter. "I doubt it's a joke." I shrugged, "Do you at least like them?"

I nodded, "They're pretty. My mom loved Tulips. My dad would always buy her the red and yellow ones." I smiled to myself. "Do you know what the colors mean?"

"The red ones are a declaration of love." He said.

"Yeah," I nodded. "The yellow ones are 'hopelessly in love' at least that's what my dad told me." a smile spread across Derek's face. "I wonder who's declaring their love for me." I laughed.

"Any guesses?"

"I'm still set on Scott playing a joke on me, so no. But I'll keep you updated." I said.

He sighed. "Okay." He turned to the freezer pulling out some chicken. "Chicken Alfredo for dinner?"

"Sounds good."

--

Derek POV

I can't believe he thought the flowers were a joke. Seriously? A joke? Why would someone play a joke on him like that? I sighed as I made dinner. Stiles was sitting on the counter across from me humming to himself as he played on his phone.

"Her Der?" I turned to look at him, "What's your middle name?"

"Tyler. Why?" I asked.

He shrugged, "Just curious."

"What's yours?" I asked, "Your first name."

He laughed, "Here." He said typing away on his phone. A few seconds later my phone went off.

From: StilesMieczysław

I looked up at him. "I like it."

"Ew. Why?" He laughed again.

"Mechi means 'sword' and slava means 'glory.'" I said.

"How'd you know that?" He smiled.

"My mom was into stuff like that."

"Then why is your name Derek?" He laughed.

"Because in older English my name is Dederick, which was in origin a Low German form of Theodoric. Theodoric is a name meaning "ruler of the people" so my mom put a lot of thought into my name." I said.

"And look at you now Mr. Alpha." Stiles smiled.

"Guess she knew me better than I know myself."

Stiles looked down, "You're pretty great, you know that?"

"Am I?" I asked.

He nodded sliding off of the counter. Walking over to me he wrapped his arms tightly around me. "I don't know what I'd do without you, Der."

I smiled hugging him back, pressing a kiss to his head.

Chapter 14

J ust a reminder for this chapter: Eye Colors

Lilac- Normal, content.Red- Physical and Mental pain.Blue- Mental Pain, sadness.Orange- Anger.Yellow- Physical Pain.Pink- Nervous, in love.

I walked inside finding Isaac in the kitchen hearing a shower on in the background.

"Who's in the shower?" I asked.

Isaac looked up from where he was cutting fruit at the island. "Stiles."

"Again?" I sighed, getting a nod in return.

"He was crying after you left."

I groaned pulling the pill bottle I got from the store out of the bag. "Deaton should be here soon." I told him getting a nod in return.

I made my way past a few of the pack members and upstairs into my room. Stiles was using my shower, again, like always. I don't mind, it's kind of nice having him in my space all the time. I found him sitting on the floor of my bathtub, his knees pulled to his chest, his head resting on top of his knees.

"Hey." I said softly seeing him lift his head and look at me.

"Hi." He said softly his eyes flashing pink to yellow and finally his normal brown.

I sat on the edge of the tub, "Deaton's on his way." I said dropping a couple pills into my hand from the bottle and handing them to him.

"Praise your soul. If this doesn't work I swear to god I'm going to kill myself." He said tilting his head back into the stream of water and taking the pills.

I sat there with him for a while in silence as we waited for Deaton to get here. He eventually asked me to shut off the light, which I did, making him sigh in relief before rubbing his temples. I reached my hand over pulling out some of his pain getting hit by him because "I hate when you do that Derek, you're just hurting yourself."

Deaton checked Stiles over quickly not finding any reason to be worried. He said something about Stiles gaining a new skill or something and that's probably why he was experiencing the migraines.

"So, every time I develop some knew power, I'm gonna be in pain?" Stiles whined.

Deaton shrugged, "Quite possibly." He said handing me a bag of herbs. "This should help. I recommend putting it in tea. But be careful around it. It effects werewolves...differently."

"What do you mean differently?" I asked seeing Deaton smile and walk out.

--

I made Stiles some tea with what Deaton gave me and sat down with him and the pack to watch a movie. Stiles yawned setting the cup on the coffee table, leaning into my side.

"Der..." I looked at him. "Thank you." He smiled.

I wrapped my arm around him. "You're welcome."

Isaac POV

Most of the pack had fallen asleep during the movie except for Derek, Cora, and I. I heard Derek sigh as Cora showed me another movie silently asking if I wanted to watch it. I nodded turning back to see Derek moving out from under Stiles and head upstairs. He looked tired. I think he's starting to worry too much about things again and I just really wish I could help.

Scott and Erica woke up while the next movie was playing. Erica choosing to head upstairs and go to bed, Scott moving to sit closer to me and eventually drift back to sleep. I heard Stiles groan from the couch. Both Cora and I turned to face each other before looking at the pale boy. He was sitting up on the couch with his eyes still closed. He yawned, rubbed his hands over his face, and pushed himself off the couch.

"Stiles?" Cora didn't get a response from the other.

I got up following Stiles as he dragged his feet across the floor and started up the stairs. He made it halfway up the staircase before whining and sitting down holding onto his head.

"Stiles, you okay?" I asked. He shook his head pulling away from me as I grabbed his arm.

I watched him blink his eyes a few times and stand back up. He let out a shaky breath and continued up the stairs. I followed him as he walked into Derek's room. The alpha was asleep in his bed, his back showing to the room, face buried in his pillow. Stiles pulled at the blanket climbing in bed and pushing himself under one of the others arms waking him up. Derek yawned looking at the smaller male. I heard a whimper come from Stiles and saw Derek kiss his temple, wrapping his arms around the younger boy.

"You want more tea?" Derek said softly, barely audible to me.

Stiles curled closer to him. "No, hold me." He replied.

I smiled sadly walking out of the doorway and back downstairs where Cora was waiting for me.

"Is he okay?"

I shrugged, "Derek's got him though." I said seeing her smile.

--

Third Person

Derek woke up when he felt Stiles tossing and turning next to him in the bed. He tried to talk to him and get him to calm down.

"Stiles, its okay, I'm right here. Come on, wake up." He mumbled, cursing himself for not knowing how to help the younger boy out of his night terror.

His attempts failed time and time again until the younger boy woke up screaming, tears covering his face. Derek wrapped him in a hug, rocking the two back and forth, calming the terrified teen as the rest of the pack made their own appearances in the room.

Scott was the first to sit down on Derek's bed. Something nobody normally dared to do but right now he didn't care. His best friend was crying and having trouble breathing.

"Stiles?" He said softly, the other looked up at him from where is head was resting against Derek's arm. "You need to control your breathing, okay?" Stiles shook his head. Scott glanced at Derek who looked just about as terrified as Stiles did. "Just match your breathes with Derek's. Can you try that?" Stiles closed his eyes trying to match the rise and fall of Derek's chest eventually calming down and relaxing in the wolf's arms.

The rest of the pack walked over crowding the boy making sure he was okay before forcing a 'puppy pile' onto the two who were still wrapped up together. Stiles squirmed around getting comfortable on Derek, Scott squished up beside him, Cora squished next to Derek, Isaac covering all four of them. The other members found a spot and laid in silence as Derek spoke up.

"Are you okay?" He asked quietly.

Stiles let out a sigh, "Yeah."

"Do you want to talk about it?" The alpha asked.

Stiles shook his head, pressing a kiss to Derek's jaw. "Just hold me." He whispered reaching back to find Scott's hand.

Stiles POV

Flashes. Glimpses. The small scenes scattering my brain causing so much pain and strife.

Screaming scattered the area.

Blood painted the walls.

I watched it. All of it. And I did nothing to stop it. Nothing to help.

The trees all pass by in a blur, like someone's running through them, like I'm running through them, like I'm being chased.

More flashes. Faces I've never seen. Faces I wished I hadn't just seen.

More screams.

More blood.

"Stiles, GO!" I turned to see Derek, a pipe going straight through his chest. He howls in pain.

"Derek!" I yell. Hands wrap around my neck and mouth.

I see Scott and Isaac tied up in the corner, unconscious.

I see Cora crying as they force her to watch her brother slowly being killed.

I see Erica being forced to stab Boyd with a knife as she cries out.

I see Allison and Lydia screaming, covered in blood, tears running down their faces.

I see Jackson lifeless on the ground.

I see the twins. Chained up. Cut open. Not healing.

"YOU DID THIS!" They all screech.

Chapter 15

'H ey Stiles!' Laura smiled.

I sat down across from her sending a smile toward her. I feel like it has been forever since I've visited with her and honestly I don't want to leave. I'm so tired all the time and I'm still in so much pain. It's been like a week since these migraines have started and there's only so much Derek and Deaton can do to help.

We sat together for a while not really talking about anything in particular. She started telling me how Derek, Cora, and her used to have movie nights. They'd lay out a bunch of blankets and pillows in the living room and get a bunch of junk food and pile up a stack of movies. They'd spend the entire weekend watching the movies until every single one had been finished.

'Derek's favorite movie is Finding Nemo. He won't admit it, but it is.' She told me.

I yawned, opening my eyes. I heard the shower on in the bathroom in Derek's room and sighed rolling over to shove my face into his pillow. I could hear him humming in the shower softly. I smiled, he's adorable sometimes. I pushed myself off the bed and grabbed the blankets off his bed along with the pillows and throwing them down the stairs before marching into my room and doing the same thing.

I started spreading the blankets out with help from Cora when Derek finally came downstairs. I heard him snort and ask "What are you doing?" Cora smiled at me.

"We're gonna have a movie day." I said as Isaac walked in with the first of many bowls of popcorn being made.

The rest of the pack made their way into the living room and onto the pile of blankets on the floor. They each had picked out a movie and placed it in a pile grabbing some sort of candy and got comfortable. I put in the first movie seeing Derek sit up against the couch next to Cora.

"Was this your idea?" I heard him ask her quietly.

"No, it's all him."

I turned around and made my way to sit next to Derek. "How's your head?" He asked wrapping an arm around me.

I shrugged, leaning into him. "Laura said 'hi.'" I said as Finding Nemo started playing on the screen.

I felt Derek tense next to me for a moment before leaning over and pressing a kiss to the side of my head. I smiled seeing Cora lean into Derek's other side and the older male pull her closer. I watched them share another glance at each other before turning my attention to the movie and enjoying the tea Deaton gave me.

--

I woke up a few hours later to see the rest of the pack had also fallen asleep. I yawned checking the time on my phone before noticing that Isaac was the only one not in the living room. I got up going to grab the pizza parlors take out menu from the kitchen to order some stuff for dinner for everyone. When I walked into the kitchen I saw Isaac sitting at the table with his head resting on his arms.

"Hey, you okay?" I asked, he shook his head slightly. "What's wrong?"

"I don't feel good." I rolled my eyes at his vague answer.

"What doesn't feel good?"

He sighed. "Everything."

"What'd you eat today?" I asked.

"Same thing everyone else did." He answered.

I bit the inside of my cheek opening one of the drawers to pull out one of the menus when I saw the bag of what Deaton gave me. "Isaac?" I turned to look at him.

"Yeah?"

"Did you drink my tea?"

He picked his head up and turned to look at me. "I...uh...I might have. I don't remember. Why?"

"Like, today? That cup I had in the living room. Did you drink out of it?"

He looked down as if he was thinking before he nodded. I sighed walking into the living room and waking Derek up. I watched him rub his hand over his face before finally looking at me with a yawn.

"What?" Sleep laced his voice.

"Isaac drank my tea." He looked at me dumbly for a few moments. "The one Deaton told you to be careful with because it 'effects wolves different-ly'." I said seeing it finally click.

"Shit." He said moving his arm from under Cora. "Where is he?"

"Kitchen."

I followed Derek into the kitchen hearing a whine from the older male. I looked down to see a little wolf cub sitting where Isaac was just minutes ago.

"I think we have a problem." I laughed.

Derek shot a glare toward me before bending down and letting Isaac sniff him before picking the cub up. "We should take him to see Deaton."

I nodded, Derek holding Isaac as a little wolf cub was the most adorable thing I've ever seen in my entire life and I couldn't hold in the squeal I made when Isaac pushed his muzzle into Derek's neck.

I smiled at Derek as he rolled his eyes and walked toward the front door. "Derek!" I followed. "Wait! I want a picture!" He ignored me opening the front door and walking outside. "It's too cute! Let me take a picture!!"

Chapter 16

This is what Isaac looks like as a cub.

Deaton explained that over time Isaac will turn back. We don't know how long it will take or if there is some type of trigger to make him change back. But he will. So, there's nothing to really worry about. Plus, he's super cute as a wolf. He's got like an ashy-light brown fur and the most adorable face ever.

I woke up seeing Derek wasn't in bed and his alarm clock said it was nearing eleven-thirty. Breakfast sounds good. I sighed pushing myself off the bed and walked down the stairs. I smiled seeing Derek was laying on his stomach on the couch. Cora was laying on the other couch with Isaac curled up by her feet. And out of everything they could be watching, they put in Nemo again. The movie was at the part where they go on a field trip and see the boat. I laughed getting Cora's attention and jumped onto Derek grabbing his butt.

"I touched the butt!" I yelled making Derek snort. Cora laughed and turned her attention back to the TV.

Derek turned managing to keep me still sitting on him. "Hey."

"Hi." I smiled. "You didn't wake me up."

He yawned, "I know. You seemed tired last night so I just let you sleep."

I hummed slipping into the space between the couch and Derek, resting my head on his chest. Isaac whined and jumped off of the couch. He looked back and forth between Cora and Derek and I.

"Cor, let Isaac out." Derek said.

Isaac jumped his little paws tapping against the wood floor as he ran down the hallway.

Cora groaned. "Why don't you ever take care of him?"

"He's been a wolf cub for like two seconds. Don't be so dramatic." Derek fought back wrapping his arm around me.

I snorted, "Okay, children."

Cora rolled her eyes but walked off without another word.

"You wanna go out for dinner tonight?" Derek asked.

"Sure." I yawned. "I'm gonna take a nap."

Derek chuckled as I cuddled in closer to him. "You just got up."

"Shh, go back to watching Nemo."

Derek didn't answer but he totally rolled his eyes at me.

--

"So, where we going?" Erica asked walking into my room.

I looked up at her, "What do you mean?"

"Dinner? Derek said something about going out."

"Oh." I thought he just meant us. No, of course he didn't mean just us. Why would he want to go to dinner with just me? We might be closer now but I'm still just Stiles. "I don't know. Ask him."

"You okay?" She asked sitting down on my bed next to me.

I nodded. "Yeah, just tired."

"Do you still have those migraines?"

I nodded again, "They're getting better. I still haven't learned anything new though so I'm kind of doubting what Deaton said." I shrugged. "I'm probably just dying."

Erica hit me. "Shut up Batman. I'm sure you'll be the most powerful angel ever. Just give it some time."

"Thanks, Catwomen." She smiled kissing my cheek and walking out of my room.

'I'm so stupid.' I thought to myself. 'Me and Derek? That would never work.'

'Ugh, seriously?' I laid back onto my bed and rubbed my eyes.

'Stiles?'

I sat up. 'What the fuck was that?'

There was a knock on my doorframe. I turned to see Scott. "Seriously what?"

"What?" I asked.

Scott scrunched his eyebrows together. "I was walking past and you said 'ugh, seriously?'"

I shook my head. "N-no, I thought that."

"Well...I heard it."

"What the fuck." I rubbed my hands over my face. "I need a nap."

Scott snorted. "You always need a nap. Come on, we're getting ready to leave."

I pushed myself off of my bed and followed Scott downstairs. Derek was pulling on his jacket with a scowl on his face. Isaac was whining up at the pack.

"I'll be here with you, calm down." Lydia groaned.

"You're not coming?"

She shook her head, "I got a huge paper due. The quiet will help. Bring me something back though." She winked and made her way to the kitchen.

I heard the front door slam shut and jumped seeing everyone still around except Derek.

"Is he okay?" Jackson asked.

Cora shrugged. "He's always moody. You guys know this." She opened the front door leaving it open as she walked out to the driveway.

I handed my keys to Scott. "I'm gonna ride with Derek."

Scott nodded,"Careful, he bites."

I snorted. "Really? That's what you came up with?"

Scott laughed, "Come on, let's go."

--

The ride was eerily quiet. Derek hadn't even so much as glanced at me. Cora was in the backseat, her headphones blaring music loud enough I could make out what song it was.

I bit my lip and closed my eyes. 'Are you mad at me?' I tried. I wasn't sure I had done it right until I heard Derek snort.

'No.' I got back.

I rubbed my hands against my pants. 'What's wrong?'

'Nothing.'

'Derek, please just tell me.'

He hadn't answered back. I reached over to grab his hand. He squeezed mine back for a short second before pulling away. I frowned.

We made it to the restaurant after what felt like an eternity in silence. Cora abandoned us immediately running to catch up to the rest of the pack. I grabbed onto Derek's arm.

"Can you just talk to me?"

Derek sighed, looking at me. "What do you want me to say?"

"Oh, I don't know? Maybe why you're being all broody and giving me the cold shoulder? You asked if I wanted to go out to dinner and now you won't even look at me."

Derek rubbed a hand over his face. "Yeah, I asked you to dinner. Then you went and invited the pack. If you didn't want to go out you could've just said no."

"What? No. I didn't invite them? Erica said that you said something to her about it."

Derek shook his head. "No, I asked you and then Erica came into my room and said you told her to ask where we were going to dinner because the pack wanted to know."

"I told her to ask you because I thought you invited the pack." I frowned.

"No, I just wanted to spend time with you."

I looked down. "I'm sorry."

"No, Stiles. It's fine. Let's just go inside. Okay?" He said grabbing my hand.

We found where the pack was sitting. 'I'd rather spend time with just you.'

I looked over to see Derek looking at me. He smiled, wrapping his arm around my shoulders. 'I guess it's not that bad though.'

I looked around the table. Scott and Jackson were playing tic tac toe on the paper placemats they had. Cora was laughing at something Aiden said. Danny and Ethan were talking. Allison, Erica, and Boyd were all in some deep conversation. Well, mostly Allison and Erica. I leaned into Derek more, my head dropping onto his shoulder. Scott's gaze met mine and he gave me a soft smile before looking back at the placemat in front of him.

'No, it's not that bad.'

Chapter 17

D erek POV

I rubbed my face feeling a weight on my chest. I smiled, taking a deep breath, and opened my eyes. Stiles was still asleep. The sunrise leaking in through the window illuminating his pale skin. I let my fingers dance along his back, from mole to mole. He let out yawn, curling into me more. It's mornings like this that I loved most. When I wake up and Stiles is in my room, not his, I don't have to get up right away and do something, there's nothing going on that I need to worry about. I craved mornings like this, although they didn't happen that often.

"Mornin' Der." Stiles' muffled voice vibrated against my chest.

I smiled. "Morning, Stiles."

He wrapped his arm around my torso, tightening his grip in a hug, and letting his arm relax across me. "I'm cold." He mumbled.

"We should get up."

He pulled the blanket up more, yawning again. "Nope. We're staying here all day."

I snorted, "Is that so?"

"Yup." He said, rubbing his nose against my jawline. "Until dinner at least. Then we're gonna go out. Just us."

"You paying?" I joked.

He nodded, "Go back to sleep."

I let out a puff of laughter, burying my nose into his hair. He was starting to fall back asleep. I wrapped my arms around him, running my hand up and down his back again.

Just us doesn't sound too bad.

--

"Derek!" I woke up to banging on my door and Scott yelling from the other side. "Derek! We have a problem!"

I got out of bed as Stiles pushed himself up so he was leaning against the headboard. "What's wrong?" I asked opening my bedroom door.

"There's a group of hunters headed this way."

I sighed, nodding. "Give me two minutes." I closed the door going over to my closet.

"Derek." Stiles whined.

I pulled my shirt over my head. "Stay here."

"What? No!"

"I don't want you getting hurt."

He snorted, "I'm not a fragile little human anymore, Derek."

"You're right, doesn't mean I want to watch you get shot by some fucking hunter though."

Stiles pushed himself out of my bed and grabbed one of my shirts. "I'm not just going to sit here like a potato." He snapped.

"Babe-" He cut me off.

"No, I'm not just sitting here." He pulled on his jeans and left the room.

I groaned as I finished getting dressed and walked downstairs.

"What the hell do you want?" I walked into the front yard where the hunters were gathered.

A tall brunette shook her head. "Nothing much, Derek."

"This isn't your territory. What the hell are you doing in Beacon Hills?"

"We just wanted to visit our favorite wolf pack. Although, seems like most of them are gone...wouldn't you say?" She looked over at an older man behind her.

I growled, "Go back to New York, we didn't do anything. You have no reason to be here."

"Actually, we do. Your father owes us. Quite a bit actually, and since he's obviously no longer around, we just decided to come straight to you instead."

"My father doesn't owe you shit."

She laughed, "Your father owes us your life, Derek."

I felt Stiles grab onto my arm, "Derek, what are they talking about?"

"You don't know?" She gasped, "We saved Talia, and little Cora over there awhile back. In return, we were supposed to get Derek over here. Kinda like a pet. But, Mr. Grumpy's dad had to go and die on us before the agreement was signed off on. We'd still like our reward though."

I growled, pushing Stiles behind me. She rolled her eyes as several more hunters appeared from various spots in the woods. All of the pulling out arrows and guns, all aimed toward my pack and I.

--

Stiles POV

"NO!" I yelled, pushing myself around Derek.

The noise seemed to stop, the breeze was gone, the birds weren't making any noise. When I looked up everyone was frozen in their spots.

"Oh my god, I broke time." I mumbled walking around everyone. "This could be super good, or super bad..." I walked toward one of the hunters. "I'll just take this..." I mumbled, pulling the gun from his grasp.

I managed to get the weapons away from every hunter except one. As I reached the last one my back started hurting where my wings come out. I rolled my shoulder and pulled off Derek's shirt letting them stretch their full length. Not even a moment after I felt an excruciating pain and was knocked to the ground as everything started moving again.

"What the hell?" I heard some of the hunters mutter.

I heard Derek growl and saw him tackle the girl who had the last gun. The fighting continued as I felt the pain spreading throughout my body. The humans no longer having their weapons gave the pack the advantage they need. I turned my head to see Scott beating the crap out of someone just as everything started to go black.

Chapter 18

S tiles POV

Everything was fuzzy when I woke up. It was almost like waking up after being under anesthetic when getting your wisdom teeth out. I groaned, rolling over to see Derek staring down at me.

"Hi." I said softly.

He smiled, "How you feeling?"

"What happened?"

"You got shot."

I nodded, "How much of my pain did you take?" He looked down, silent. "Thanks, Der." I moved to lay my head in his lap. His fingers began raking through my hair, silence engulfing the room comfortably.

There was a loud knock at the door. Derek groaned and let out a 'What?' as the door opened.

Cora stood in the doorway as Isaac walked in, still stuck as a cub. "He won't stop whining." She said.

Derek turned helping the little wolf on the bed. The older male frowned as he took some of Isaac's pain.

"Do you think he's just shifting back? I mean he didn't feel good before he changed." I asked sitting up, squeezing my eyes in pain. My wings weren't out but the pain was still very much there.

Cora sat at the end of the bed. "I don't know." Derek responded. "You can go to bed. I'll keep an eye on him." He looked at his sister.

She nodded, "Love you." She called bounding out of the room, Derek responding as he pet Isaac's head.

"If he's still not okay in the morning I'm gonna take him to Deaton's."

I nodded, resting my head on his shoulder. "Do you think I could talk to him? Like in his head? Would it work?"

"I don't know." Derek responded.

'Can you hear me?' I asked waiting to see if it worked. Isaac stood up and nudged my knee with his head.

'Is that a yes?' Isaac licked my hand. "Der, I don't think he can respond."

"Do you feel sick like before you turned?" Isaac whined.

I looked at Derek who sighed and pulled the cub into his lap. Isaac let out a long whine making Derek frown. "I'm sorry Is. We'll see Deaton tomorrow." Isaac licked Derek's hand curling into him more.

I don't remember anything after that.

Chapter 19

"S tiles...Stiles...oh my god, STILES!"

I groaned, "What the hell do you want, Is, I'm sleeping."

"Derek told me to wake you up."

"No." I pulled the covers up around me more, "Wait..." I sat up. "You're not a cub anymore!?"

Isaac laughed, "No, I woke up this morning...well...like this."

I nodded, the sound from the shower finally registering in my brain, "Derek in the shower?"

"Yeah, we're going to see Deaton."

"Okay...but you had to wake me up...why?"

"Because, you're going." Isaac said.

I snorted, "No, I'm not."

"Stiles, you got shot. You're going." I turned to see Derek walking out of his bathroom. Water dripped off of his hair and down his face. "Got it?" I watched the droplet make its way down his neck and chest, my eyes roaming toward his hips where he had his towel wrapped around him. "Stiles, my eyes are up here."

I felt my face heat up, "I know, I just...shut up."

Isaac snorted, "I'll be downstairs."

Derek watched Isaac walk out before turning toward his dresser, "I like when your eyes turn pink."

"Why?" I felt my cheeks heat up again.

"Because you only do it around me." He pulled out a pair of boxers.

"I-I uh...I do?" He nodded, "I don't notice when they change."

He smiled, "I didn't think so, they're pretty when they change, like now."

"Now?"

Derek nodded, "They're still pink."

I watched him walk into the bathroom, the door closing behind him for a few moments, he walked back out in his boxers, "Although, your brown eyes are my favorite."

"Thanks..." I whispered, dropping my head.

"Come on, get dressed."

I groaned but got up, "Fine, but I'm wearing one of your sweaters." Derek just hummed in response.

--

We got to Deaton's shortly after Derek was talking to him, Isaac sat himself on the metal table, legs swinging, eyes locked onto the other two in front of him. I rubbed my eyes, it felt as if the room around me was starting to spin. I grabbed onto Derek's arm getting his attention.

"What's wrong?" I faintly heard before everything went black.

"Stiles." I turned around to see my mom standing behind me.

"Mom?" She smiled sitting down. "What's going on?"

"I wanted to talk to you." I nodded waiting for her to continue. "How are you?"

"Um...fine? I mean, I was shot the other day but it's getti-"

She cut me off, "I didn't mean physically. Mentally, how are you."

"I'm fine, why?"

She grabbed onto my hand, "It's just a big adjustment, I want to make sure you're okay."

"I'm fine, mom, promise."

"Just remember, you have people down there who care about you even if they don't always say it."

I nodded, "I know."

"I love you, honey."

"I love you too, mom."

My mom faded away and I sat there alone for a few seconds before Laura appeared.

"Hey, Stiles."

"Hi."

"Question." I looked up, "Did you and my brother finally get your shit together?"

I scrunched my eyebrows together, "What're you talking about?"

"Your disgusting crushes. Are you guys together yet?" I didn't answer her, my gaze on her breaking as I rubbed my head. "Headache?" I nodded, "Yeah, that happens the first few times you get forced up here." She laughed.

"Is that all you wanted?"

She nodded, "More or less. Is he doing okay?"

"I think so."

"Okay, don't hurt him." She sighed. "He loves you, ya know."

I gave a small smile as she continued, "Just, make the first move or something, okay? I'm sick of you guys dancing around each other like it's not obvious."

I snorted, "I'll think about it. Can I go back now?"

"I suppose." She groaned dramatically, fondness was drawn across her face though.

"Stiles, Stiles wake up."

"Derek, he passed out just give him a minute."

I forced my eyes open, Derek was crouched down in front of me, "I'm okay, Der."

He pulled me into a hug, "Are you sure?"

"Yes," I laughed, "My mom and Laura just wanted to talk to me."

"Laura? About what?"

I shrugged, "Help me up?" he pulled me up, "Is Isaac okay?"

"Yeah, he's in the car."

"What about me?"

Deaton finally spoke up, "I need to see your wing still."

I nodded, "Right, um..." I pulled off Derek's sweater, one of my wings knocked some of the jars on the counter over. "I'm sorry...they're not fit for small spaces."

"I got it." Derek said, walking over.

"Don't touch any of that." Deaton snapped. "Werewolves."

I laughed at Derek's sour expression toward the others comment. He looked over my wing, rubbing some type of cream on it and putting a bandage over top.

"It's healing well, this will help with the pain, help it heal. I suggest letting your wings out every couple hours, give it some time to breathe while it heals. It'll make it less painful, it'll heal faster that way too."

"Okay, thanks Doc."

Deaton nodded, "Anytime, Stiles."

"Can we get food?" I turned toward Derek, retracting my wings. He nodded, I pulled the sweater back on and hummed happily. "Cool." I said kissing his cheek and walking out of the back room.

When Derek finally walked out of the car there was a blush covering his face and he looked uncomfortable.

"You okay?"

He nodded, "Deaton's...full of information I didn't need to know." He said, grabbing my hand. "Where do you want to eat?"

Isaac spoke from the backseat, "God, I'm starving."

Their voices were drown out by my thoughts, the only thing I could focus on was the feel of Derek's thumb rubbing across the back of my hand.

"You okay?" Derek broke my thoughts. I nodded. "Is that café down the street good?"

I nodded, "Perfect."

Chapter 20

S tiles pressed a kiss to my cheek, his eyes flashing pink before he made his way out of the building. Deaton was smirking at me the entire time.

"Shut up." He raised his hands in defense with a laugh.

"He loves you." I rolled my eyes at him. "Seriously Derek, he does."

"So, what's your point?"

Deaton shrugged, "You should tell him how you feel."

"And why would I do that?"

"Because the full moons coming up." I raised my eyebrow at him. "You could do that mating ritual? Claim him?"

I groaned, "You want me to 'werewolf marry' Stiles? Even if I wanted that, I wouldn't spring that on him yet. The full moon's in less than a week. That's a lot on any relationship let alone one that isn't even existent."

"He might want it too."

"I don't care. Even if we were together I wouldn't do that this soon. It's unethical."

Deaton shrugged, "It'd be just as good for him as it would be for you, Derek."

"What are you talking about?"

He shook his head, "Nothing, go on. The boys are hungry."

"No, they're fine. What the hell are you going on about?"

Deaton sighed, "Angels have mates too Derek, he's feeling everything you are. He wants to mate just as bad as you do."

"Why does it matter if he does? Our relationship is between us? Why do you care?"

"I don't," He started. "But like I said before, if he feels unwanted, he'll stop saving you, and from what I could tell he's heading down the wrong path."

"What am I supposed to do?"

"Fix it."

--

"You okay?" Stiles' voice caught my attention. I nodded babbling some response asking where he wanted to eat. Isaac mumbled from the backseat, I watched Stiles look out the window, his eyes flashed red and he shifted like he was in pain.

"You okay?" I parroted to him, my hand finding its way to his.

He nodded, agreeing to the café down the road and his gaze set itself out the window again, he squeezed my hand slightly as I drove.

I kept glancing over at him, how was I supposed to fix this? Even if I do something about this...thing going on with us that doesn't mean he's going to feel any different. Not if he's feeling like this because of the pack.

--

"Hey Der?" Stiles asked, walking into my bedroom.

I looked up from the book in front of me, "Yeah?"

"Wanna play Mario Kart with me?"

I raised my eyebrow at him, "What happened to Scott?"

Stiles shrugged, "He's 'busy' so, you wanna play?"

"Not really." I laughed.

"Come on, please!? All you do is read, aren't you kind of bored of it yet?"

"No," I snorted as I got up, "But if it'll make you happy I'll play."

A smile painted across his face. "Really? Yay!" He said, jumping a little.

I made my way downstairs and sat on the couch. He walked out of the kitchen with a can of Pepsi and a Beer. He handed me the Beer and a controller before plopping himself on the floor in front of me.

"Okay, so you can pick which one you want first, just not rainbow road, got it?"

I snorted, "Why not?"

"That one was created by Satan himself."

"Okay, fine." I leaned forward, my elbows rested on my knees, arms around Stiles' shoulders. "What about this one?"

He snorted, "Can you handle that one?" the cocky tone in his voice made me smirk.

"Let's find out."

A half an hour passed before Stiles groaned, head leaning back into my lap to look up at me.

"I can't prove it, but I know you're cheating."

I laughed, "Don't be a sore loser just because you undermined my video game abilities."

"That was the nerdiest thing you've ever said." He smiled.

I leaned down and pecked his lips, standing up and tossing the controller on the couch. "What do you want for dinner?" I asked walking toward the kitchen.

Stiles appeared in front of me. "You can't just do that and then walk away!"

"Since when can you do that?"

"Do what?"

"Teleport yourself?"

He smirked, "New trick." His face turning serious again. "But seriously, you can't just kiss me and then walk away!"

"Why not?"

"Wh-!? You can't be serious?"

I just stared at him, his eyes hadn't changed color and I was kind of happy because his brown eyes will always be my favorite. A blush rose on his cheeks as I continued to look at him.

"What are you looking at?" He scoffed, the skip in his heart beat didn't go unnoticed.

I shook my head lightly at him and smiled, "You."

He dropped his head, a smile on his face. I lifted his chin, "Dinner, what do you want?"

He snorted pressing his lips against mine, "Chinese. Make the call quick, I need to beat your werewolf ass in the near future."

"Okay." I said softly, pecking his lips again. He hit my chest playfully letting out a quiet "stop" and bounded back into the living room.

"Hey, Sourwolf?" Stiles asked when I walked back over. "Did it hurt when you fell from heaven?"

I sighed rolling my eyes and sitting back down on the couch, he got up sitting next to me.

"Because you're literally Lucifer."

"There's no need for such flattery."

Stiles snorted. "Wow, you can be funny."

I smiled a little pulling him closer to me, "Start the stupid game, loser."

"Fine."

I let him win (but he's too cocky to realize it).

Chapter 21

Reminder: Eye Colors

Lilac- Normal, contentRed- Physical pain and Mental PainBlue- Mental pain, SadnessOrange- AngerYellow- Physical PainPink- Nervous, in love

This bounces through different POV's a bit but hang in there with me.

Stiles POV

I woke up noticing Derek wasn't in bed anymore. Yawning, I kicked off the covers and climbed out of bed, I pulled on a pair of his sweatpants and one of his sweatshirts before making my way downstairs. When I found him, he was pacing in the living room, most of the pack was sitting down watching the scene in front of them.

"What's going on?" I asked, leaning on the doorframe.

Scott looked up nodding for me to come over. I sat next to him, he mumbled something about a threat but Derek hasn't given much information to anyone about it yet. He just started pacing, phone clutched in his hand. I sighed, looking around, Allison, Isaac, and Scott were curled up together on the couch next to me. Erica and Boyd were sitting together in the arm chair. Lydia and Jackson were leaning against the wall. Cora, Aiden, Ethan, and Danny were in a big bundle leaning against the couch. I looked back up at Derek who finally stopped pacing. He stood eerily still, phone clutched in his hand as he bit on his nails.

"Fuck!" He snapped, walking out, the front door slamming made everyone jump.

I climbed over the back of the couch to follow him, he walked past the Camaro and up the driveway. "Derek!" I called grabbing onto his elbow.

He pulled out of my grasp continuing to walk away as I called his name again. He was muttering under his breath when I grabbed onto his hand. "Derek! Talk to me!"

"No! Go away Stiles!" He snapped at me, pulling his hand away.

"I just want to help..." I said quietly, the harsh look on his face breaking my heart.

"I don't want your help." His words piercing me with venom as he turned and continued walking away.

I squeezed my eyes feeling a tear roll down my face, "fine." I pulled off his sweatshirt letting it fall to the ground as I let my wings out.

"Stiles!" I heard Derek yell as I took off, the crisp morning air cold against my skin but still more pleasant than how I was feeling inside. If he didn't want my help then I won't give it to him.

Derek POV

"H-He just took off!" I muttered to Scott.

"Derek, relax." Scott said. "What happened?"

I balled my hands into fists, "I-I yelled at him. I didn't mean to, but I did. Fuck, Scott I-"

"Hey, Derek, look at me. He's just upset. We'll find him. We'll bring him home."

Cora wrapped herself around me, "It'll be okay big brother." She said as I hugged her back.

"I-I didn't mean to...Scott...I-I didn't..."

"I know. Relax." Scott sighed, "Where would Stiles go if he wanted to be alone?"

"His house?" Lydia offered.

Jackson spoke up after, "What about the school? He used to practice when he got upset?"

"Graveyard?" Erica said.

Scott nodded, "Let's split up. I have an idea of where he might be. Derek, stay here in case he comes back, Cora you too, he probably won't want to see Derek."

"Are you making me the buffer?"

"Yes." Scott stated. "Lydia, Jackson, go to the school. Erica, Boyd, Ethan, Danny, go to Stiles' old house. Aiden, Allison, Isaac, check the graveyard."

"Where are you going?" Allison asked.

He shook his head, "We have this spot, we don't go there much but when my dad left and after his mom...it was our spot. I think he might be there."

Scott POV

When I showed up to the spot Stiles and I share I saw him sitting on the big rock that sat in the middle of a bunch of trees, there's a lake just in front. I pulled off my sweatshirt draping his across his bare torso as I sat next to him. He looked at me for a moment before dropping his head onto my shoulder.

"He yelled at me."

I sighed, "I know. He didn't mean to."

Stiles let out a harsh laugh sitting up again, "yes he did, everyone means it."

"What're you talking about?"

"I'm just a burden, I should've stayed dead." He muttered.

I hit his arm, "That's not fucking true you asshole. We need you, we love you, and you're not even close to a burden to any of us."

"Doesn't feel that way."

"Stiles," he stopped me.

"Can we just not do this right now?" He asked, "Please?"

I sighed, wiped his cheek, and pulled him into a hug. "Come home."

"In a little..." He whispered turning to look back toward the lake "Stay?"

"Always."

--

Third Person

Scott texted the pack letting them know he had found Stiles. The two of them not coming home till after dinner time. They walked to Scott's car, arms linked together, Stiles pulling Scott's jacket around him tighter as it got colder.

Derek pulled Stiles into a hug as soon as they walked through the door, "I'm sorry, I didn't mean it." He muttered, the words falling out of the wolf's mouth and onto the floor.

"It's fine, I don't want to talk about it right now." Stiles said quietly, pulling away from him.

Derek's wolf whined when Stiles' eyes flashed blue before he stalked off.

"Just leave him be tonight, you can talk to him tomorrow." Scott said.

Derek nodded, "I'm going to bed."

They didn't sleep in the same bed that night, Stiles locked in his room, Derek in his. The pack could feel the tension floating through the house, Scott trying to assure everyone that everything would be fine soon. It'd all be fine.

Chapter 22

The knock on Stiles' door made him jump, he turned to see Derek standing in the doorway. He sighed closing his laptop and turning toward the older man.

"I'm sorry, I didn't mean to yell at you I'm just kind of stressing out and...I just...snapped." Stiles nodded waiting for Derek to continue, "There's two packs threatening ours and I'm going to explain it all when the rest of the pack get here but...Stiles I'm sorry."

The younger gave him a small smile, "It's fine, I was probably being over-dramatic." He shrugged.

"You weren't be dramatic, you were upset. Because of me. I...god I'm so sick of upsetting everyone." Derek muttered more to himself than the boy in front of him.

"What're you talking about, Derek?"

He shook his head in response, "It's not important. Like I said, I'll explain more when the pack gets here."

"Okay."

Stiles watched as the other walked out of his sight before he let out a sigh and slouched a bit.

'Seriously, what the hell was that?' he thought to himself.

--

The pack watched their alpha fidgeting in front of them, silence eerily invading the room, his eyes kept darting to Stiles and down at his feet and then up at Cora and back to his feet repeating the process a few times before he sighed and began to speak.

"Two packs threatened ours." He started, "One of them I'm not familiar with, but I know they're powerful. The other..." He turned to look at Cora. "You're other pack wants you back."

"What, why?" She asked, confusion falling into the open air.

Derek sighed, "They don't think I'm a fit enough alpha to be protecting you."

"What the hell are they talking about?"

"They're referring to my beta eyes." Derek said quietly.

A whine escaped Isaac's mouth upon hearing what Derek said, "That wasn't your fault."

Derek looked away not responding to Isaac, Cora trying her best not to throw a fit from her spot on the couch knowing it wasn't Derek's fault.

"What about the other pack? What do they want?" Scott broke the tension in the room.

"Stiles." Derek answered.

Stiles looked up from where his eyes were glued to his hands, "What? Me? Why?"

"It's getting out that you're an angel, a Guardian. You're going to be wanted by a lot of packs."

"That's not fair, why can't they just get their own angel." Stiles grumbled.

Cora snorted, "There aren't many other angels you dumbass."

"Rude." Stiles muttered.

"Wait, so Stiles is like a rare type of supernatural?" Erica asked.

Derek nodded, "As far as I know, he's the only angel in the United States. The few that I know about are located in Europe."

"There's one in Australia." Cora added. "But adding them all up, including Stiles, there can't be more than five angels on earth at the moment."

"Woah, okay hold on. But there's like a bunch of different types of angels how can there only be like five?" Stiles blurted in disbelief.

Derek sighed, "I don't know Stiles, that's not a question we can answer. Maybe there are more but nobody knows about them."

"How'd word get out about Stiles?" Everyone turned to look at Lydia who'd been quiet the entire time she'd been there.

The alpha licked his lips, "Someone could've been passing through and sensed it, a witch—if they are close enough—would be able to sense it. There's several ways it could've gotten out and it would've eventually I just didn't think it'd be so soon."

"Great, I'm gonna die, again."

Scott elbowed Stiles, "Don't worry, I'll keep you safe." He smirked at his best friend.

"This new-found heroism is making me very attracted to you, Scotty." Stiles replied getting a few giggles from the girls.

Derek forced himself not to growl at the two, Stiles isn't his, besides it was a joke. That's how they always are together.

"I'm gonna run the preserve." Derek sighed walking out of the living room.

--

Stiles was sitting on Derek's bed when he got home, he was flipping through one of the books from Deaton he'd been given. They hadn't said a word to each other as Derek grabbed some clean clothes and made his way into his bathroom to shower. When he was finished he'd found Stiles hadn't moved from his spot. The pale boy turning his head as the bathroom door opened.

"Can I ask you something?" His voice was really quiet, Derek nodded sitting down next to him. "Why couldn't you just tell me that yesterday?"

"I just found out, I hadn't even had time to process it." He replied, "The only thing going through my mind was that I was gonna lose Cora and then I was gonna lose you and I can't, fuck Stiles I can't lose you two." Derek dropped his head, tears running down his cheeks.

Stiles grabbed Derek's face making him look over at him, "You're not going to lose either of us Bear." He said wiping the tears off the others face. "Cora doesn't want to leave and I sure as hell am not going anywhere."

Derek leaned in so his forehead was against Stiles', "You're all I really have left." He whispered.

"That's not true. Derek you have a whole pack, you rebuilt the Hale pack, that's amazing. Your family is so proud of you. Don't forget that."

"Okay." Derek whispered, bumping his nose against Stiles', the other rubbing his thumbs across Derek's cheeks.

"I'm not going anywhere." Stiles repeated, pressing a short kiss to Derek's lips.

When he pulled away Derek felt himself leaning back in not ready for the kiss to end. "Promise?"

"I promise, Derek."

Chapter 23

I woke up to Stiles running his fingers through my hair. Groaning, I leaned into the touch. Knowing that two different packs would be here any moment was so stressful and I was trying to hide that from the pack. Internally, I'm freaking out. Deep down I know that we'll be able to sit down with Cora's old pack and have a civil conversation about the whole thing, maybe afterwards there'd be some issues, a few punches thrown but nobody would get seriously hurt. The other pack though, I know nothing about and I can't stop thinking the worst. This pack could come in with the goal to wipe out my pack completely just to get to Stiles.

"Stop thinking so much." Stiles said, leaning down to kiss me.

I relaxed a little, sighing when Stiles sat back up. "Sorry."

"Everything will be fine." He patted my chest. "C'mon, let's get breakfast."

I nodded getting up, watching Stiles roll out of bed. He stood by the door in his boxers and my t-shirt from the night before. His hair was a mess and I'm pretty sure there's drool dried to his face but god, he's so fucking beautiful.

"If you don't get up now, I'm not making you any pancakes."

I smirked getting out of bed, seeing him smile as he started to walk toward the stairs. As soon as we got downstairs he turned on some music and began to sing along as he cooked. I grabbed his hand pulling him toward me, his eyes flashed pink at me as he wrapped his arms around my shoulders. My hands pulling him closer by his waist.

"You're being quite cuddly today." He said softly.

I kissed him, pulling away enough to rest my forehead against his. "Be my boyfriend." I said softly.

He gasped, "I'm not already?" He laughed. "That took you way too long."

"Is that a yes?" I asked, he nodded pecking my lips.

"But, I'm hungry so let me cook."

I let him turn back toward the stove, wrapping my arms back around him I rested my chin on his shoulder. Every part of me wants to claim him right now, but I can't do that.

--

"What can I do for you, Derek?" Deaton's voice rang over the phone.

"The Cambridge Pack threatened us."

"Do you know why?"

I sighed, "It got out that Stiles is an angel. I don't know what to do."

"I see." He said, "Well, I'm not very familiar with them so I don't know how to help you so much with that, although, I know how to get rid of the want over Stiles."

I waited for him to continue not getting anything, "Okay, and?"

"If you claim him he can't go to another pack."

"I don't know if that's something he wants though."

"Maybe that's a conversation you should have with him." Deaton sighed, "Remember Derek, he's feeling the same way you are. He might not know exactly what it is he's feeling but he's feeling it. He does want it on some level."

"Okay," I sighed, "Thanks."

The full moon's in two days, if this is going to happen, it needs to happen fast. But, how do I bring this up to him without him thinking that I only want to claim him to keep him in the pack, to keep him safe. That's not what I want, I want to claim him because he's my mate and I love him but that's not something I know how to say without possibly scaring him.

Stiles sat down next to me on the steps of the front porch, "Hi, boyfriend." He laughed.

I wrapped my arm around him, "Hi, babe."

"You're thinking again..."

"Yeah," I sighed, "We should talk."

Chapter 24

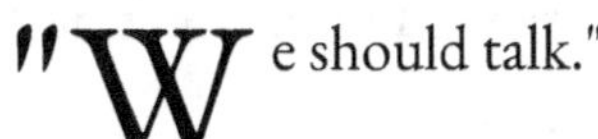

"**W**e should talk."

Stiles raised his eyebrows at me, "Well, talk then?"

"I just..." I sighed rubbing my hands together, "I don't want you to get the wrong idea."

"You're not dumping me right? Because like, I've had really short relationships but damn this would be a new record, I didn't think I was that bad of a person." He laughed, I could hear the underlying hurt in his voice though.

"What?" I asked, "No, Stiles, that's not even close to it."

"Than what is it?"

Rubbing my neck, I let out a deep breath, "If you wanted...I was kind of hoping...maybe we could do the mating ritual...and I could maybe claim you...and...yeah."

"You mean, in like a day?" He asked, "You want me to go off with you and leave our pack here, alone, so we can spend the next three days mating?"

"You don't have to if you don't want to, really, it can wait."

"Does this have something to do with that pack that wants me? Is it supposed to help or something?"

I groaned, "See, that's why I didn't want to...yes, it would help. But, that's not why I want to. I've wanted to for a while b-but, I didn't think you'd want to. And now Deaton's all on my case about it because of who knows what reason and I just kind of...I don't know."

"Derek, I don't care but it's kind of shitty timing, don't you think?"

"I know, which is another reason I didn't want to bring it up but it'd help with one part of the problem and I know that Cora's old pack won't pull any shit especially if we're doing the ritual, they're not like that."

"I just...I don't want to leave them to get hurt if we're gone. I-I'm wired to be extra protective now or something and even when they're just at their houses or at school or something I feel this overwhelming need to check in on everyone, I don't...I know they can handle themselves, but...if I'm feeling like this now and we leave them when there's two threats on us, like...I don't think it'd go over well."

I sighed, "No, I get it. It's just, I really don't know what to do right now. A-And this pack, the one that wants you, I don't know what lengths they'll go to try and get to you."

"Der, stop stressing, okay?" Stiles said, hugging me. "Let me talk to Deaton and the pack, we can figure something out. Okay? Just, you need to relax a little."

"Stiles, it's not your job to figure shit out, it's mine. I'm alpha."

"Yeah, and you're bringing up a really big topic so I think that gives me all the right in the world to take over for a bit."

--

"So, Deaton. I hear you're pressuring Derek into things." Stiles said, walking into the vet's office.

"I may have suggested a few things but I wouldn't go as far as pressuring him."

Stiles rolled his eyes, "I have some questions though, because like, I do want to do that with him, which I'm sure you knew which is why you were pressuring him a-"

"Stiles."

"Right, sorry." He sighed, "Anyways, is there any way to make the three day...in to...I don't know...a night?"

Deaton shook his head, "For the actual ritual to be completed it must take place over three days. Before the moon, during the moon, and after the moon."

"Could we just do it at home?"

Deaton nodded, "But, if you're thinking that so you can help the pack if something comes up, you're wrong. That would break the bond happening and you'd have to redo the ritual entirely."

Stiles sighed, leaning up against the table. "But, I can't just...leave them. What if they get attacked?"

"It's highly unlikely that either pack is going to come during the full moon. They both have things to worry about during this time and if I thought it would be bad timing I wouldn't have brought it up to Derek."

"But, how do I know everything will be fine?"

Deaton sighed, "You don't, but you have a strong pack and they'll be able to handle themselves for three days. I promise. If it'll help I can...do a little something, protect the house. You can have them stay there and nothing will be able to happen, okay?"

"I-I guess, I'm just worried."

"You're a Guardian, it's your job to worry."

"Yeah, well I hate it."

--

"Okay. Let's go." Stiles said, walking into Derek's room.

"Go where?"

"Didn't you pick a place for the whole ritual thing? You were supposed to pick a place, I thought you picked a place?" Stiles' heart stopped.

Derek's eyebrows raised, "Woah, calm down, I didn't even know we were doing it? We're doing it?"

Stiles nodded, "I talk to Deaton and I feel better."

"O-Okay, I uh...I'll uh..."

"Get a room." Stiles said. "You're getting a room."

"Yes, that. I'm doing that." Derek said fumbling to find his phone.

Stiles laughed, "You're phones on your dresser."

"Right, yes."

Stiles rolled his eyes climbing onto Derek's bed watching him as he paced back and forth while he was on the phone. With a yawn Stiles laid back on the bed continuing to watch Derek. As soon as Derek got off the phone he grabbed a duffel bag from his closet throwing a few things inside.

Stiles snorted, "You're packing a bag? Aren't we supposed to be naked during this whole thing??"

"No." Derek smirked, "Unless that's what you want."

Stiles climbed off the bed pulling one of Derek's sweater's from the closet, "I want this. Forever. It's mine now." He said holding it to his chest. "Kay, so I'm gonna get something to eat. You pack...and we'll leave after."

"Okay." Derek laughed, pecking the other on the lips.

Stiles smiled rubbing his nose against Derek's and walking out of the room, Derek smiled to himself when he noticed the pink fade out of Stiles' eyes.

Chapter 25

- -

Warning: horribly bad, super short smut headed your way.

Stiles walked into the room Derek had managed to get that night. He was still on edge about leaving the pack alone but he knew it was best for not only him and Derek, but the threat out against them. He sighed, listening to Derek explain how they basically couldn't leave the room or see anyone as Stiles flopped onto the bed.

"Then, how are we supposed to eat? You didn't pack any food." Stiles said, his head turning toward the bathroom.

Derek sat on the bed next to him, untying his boots. "This hotel is specifically for the supernatural and different types of mating rituals and stuff so we can order room service and it comes up this little elevator kind of thing for us."

"What the hell do mean!?" Stiles sat up.

Derek pointed to the small square door on the wall. Stiles laughed, "I'm ordering food right now. This is not real."

Derek laughed, pulling his shirt over his head. "Find something to watch while you're at it."

--

After Stiles had finished eating he pushed himself off the bed and walked toward the bathroom, squealing and running back out. "Get naked, now."

Derek snorted, "Why?"

Stiles rolled his eyes pulling Derek off the bed and dragging him into the bathroom. "Do you see that?"

"You mean the bathtub?"

"I mean, the huge bathtub that can fit more than just us and the giant wall full of bubbles and rose petals and candles and fuck Derek, we're taking a bath right now."

Derek raised his eyebrows, "Really? You want the first time you see me naked to be for a bath."

"YES!" Stiles yelled, turning the water on. "Clothes off."

Derek laughed but did as he was told climbing into the bathtub with Stiles.

"You're the best." Stiles hummed leaning into Derek.

Derek rolled his eyes.

--

"So, how does this day one work?" Stiles asked after they'd finished the bath.

"Basically, we just do whatever we want."

"I thought we were supposed to fuck."

Derek yawned, "Not till the full moon and can you not call it that."

"But, that's what it is?" Stiles laughed.

"Whatever. We don't really do much of anything."

"Can I call the pack?" He asked.

"Not after tonight." Derek said, climbing into bed.

Stiles sighed, "So, I should call now?"

"Yes." Derek yawned again, rolling onto his stomach and wrapping his arms around the pillow.

Stiles grabbed his phone, dialing Scott's number, and crawling across the bed to lay on top of Derek's bare back. He pushed his fingers through the wolf's hair as he spoke on the phone. Stiles' nerves eased a bit by the time he hung up. Derek was forcing himself to stay awake, failing miserably as he kept dozing off. Stiles tossed his phone on the bedside table and got up to shut off the light. He climbed back in bed, laying on Derek's back again.

"Goodnight, Der." Stiles hummed, his fingers dancing up and down Derek's side.

"I love you." Derek muttered back, the words mashing together with sleep, smile tracing his lips when Stiles kissed his tattoo and said the three words back to him.

--

Stiles woke up the next morning with Derek's weight on top of him. He was lying on his stomach with Derek's head in the curve of his back, the wolves arms wrapped tightly around his waist. Stiles smiled to himself before wiggling out from underneath the older man, a whine coming from the wolf, so he could go to the bathroom. Walking back out he saw Derek blinking tiredly at him, he had grabbed the pillow Stiles had been using and pulled it toward him.

"You left me." He said quietly, sleep lacing his voice.

Stiles smiled climbing onto Derek, rubbing his back. "I had to pee."

Derek let out a long sigh, "You're gross."

"Everyone pee's, Derek."

"You have the bladder of a squirrel though."

"What's that supposed to mean?"

"It means you get up at least four times a night to go pee."

Stiles hit Derek's back, "That's not my fault."

Derek laughed, "Yes, it is."

"Whatever." Stiles scoffed, "What're we supposed to do all day?"

"Nothing."

"Really? I can't even get any action from you?"

Derek snorted, rolling onto his back. "Nope. You have to wait."

"I'm bored."

Derek lifted his hand to run his fingers through the others hair, "You're so gorgeous."

Stiles' face was painted over with red, "Shut up."

Derek smiled grabbing Stiles' face and pulling him closer, "You're gorgeous." He whispered again, kissing the other. Stiles smiled against his lips letting out a soft laugh.

"You're a pain."

"Oh well." Derek smirked, pecking his lips again.

--

Derek paced around the hotel room, Stiles watching him from the bed. It was almost time. The moon was rising.

"Are you sure you want to do this?" Derek asked.

"Yes. Are you sure?"

"I-I just don't want you to regret it. Stiles, you can't turn back after it's done. We'll be mated for life. You get that right?"

Stiles sighed, getting up and pulling Derek toward the bed. "Yes, I get that. It's what I want. It's what you want. So, let's do it. Literally."

Derek nodded, "I just don't want you to be stuck with me."

"I'm not stuck with you Derek. I love you, you're my person. A-And I plan on keeping it that way for quite a while."

"I love you too." Derek's ears were burning red.

Stiles kissed him before looking out the window, "I think it's about time, Der."

Derek nodded, pulling off his shirt, pulling Stiles' off right after. Stiles smirked, pulling at Derek's sweatpants, the wolf letting the younger help him out of them. Derek pushed Stiles down onto the bed gently, pulling his pants off, his mouth finding its way to the others neck, kissing the spot where his neck and shoulder blends together.

"That's where I have to bite you."

Stiles tilted his head more, "Okay."

Derek placed a trail of kisses down the others chest, stopping to suck on his hip bone. He rubbed Stiles through his boxers, smirking as the younger let out a moan. He pulled Stiles' boxers off sucking on the younger's balls, his wolf was ecstatic at the noises Stiles was making.

"Fuck, Derek." Stiles let out as the wolf started sucking on the head of his dick.

Just before Stiles came undone, Derek pulled away. A whine breaking out of Stiles' mouth.

"What the hell?" Derek smirked, reaching over to the bedside table and grabbing a condom and lube. "No, no condom."

"Are you sure?"

"Yes. Don't you have to knot me?"

Derek sighed, "I don't know if I can."

"What?"

"I don't know if I can. That's normally for like...babies."

Stiles snorted, "So, because I can't have your babies you can't knot me?"

"I don't know. I don't know how it works. Nobody told me."

Stiles kissed Derek's nose, "Relax. I don't want a condom either way."

Derek nodded, "Okay."

Derek opened Stiles up slowly, letting the sounds of his moans burn in his memory. Stiles gave the okay, Derek covering himself in lube, moaning at the touch after being neglected, slowly pushing into Stiles. He didn't move until Stiles told him to. Going slowly the entire time. Stiles wrapped his legs around Derek's waist, his nails digging into the wolf's shoulders, they let out moans into each other's mouths as they tried and failed to give each other sloppy kisses.

"Derek, fuck." Stiles' voice raspy, his head turning toward the window. "Derek, I'm gonna...you need to claim me."

Derek kissed over the spot waiting just before Stiles was about to come to bite into his shoulder. Stiles tightened around him forcing him into his own climax. He licked over the bite, kissing it gently, trailing his kisses back up Stiles' neck to find his lips.

"I love you." Derek said softly.

"I love you too." Stiles smiled.

Okay, so my smut is always bad and I have no motivation to make it better so it's super short and worse than normal. I'm not even sorry. I am sorry about taking twelve years to update. I'm trying, I swear. I love you all so so much. I really hope you all realize how much you mean to me.

Chapter 26

Derek woke up, the sun shining through the window brightening the room. Stiles was snoring softly next to him. He smiled reaching over to get his phone off the bedside table. It was close to eleven and they'd have to leave soon. He set his phone back down and turned to wrap himself around Stiles, his chest pressed to the younger's back. He pressed soft kisses along Stiles' shoulder and up his neck, tracing kisses over the claim mark and sucking slightly on a mole that was just under Stiles' ear. His mate hummed and pushed closer to him.

"I'm sleeping." He said quietly, exhaustion lacing through his words.

Derek kissed his cheek, "Wake up."

Stiles groaned, turning in Derek's arms to push his head under the other's chin. "No."

Derek's fingers danced across Stiles' back and over the marks where his wings came out. His palm traced over the curve of his back stopping just above Stiles' ass. "You feeling better today?"

Stiles yawned, "Not as sore, still hurts a little." A whine rang up through Derek as he started to pull the pain from his mate. "Stop," Stiles grabbed his hand moving it. "I like it. It's a good pain." He smiled, finally opening his eyes to meet the wolf's gaze.

"Are you sure?"

Stiles nodded, "Reminds me that you're mine."

Derek snorted, "I've always been yours."

Stiles rubbed his nose against Derek's turning to get off the bed, Derek pulled him back pressing their lips together.

"I haven't brushed my teeth yet."

"I don't care." He smiled kissing him again.

--

Stiles stood next to Derek, arms wrapped around the older male's arm as he checked out. When it was done Stiles dropped Derek's arm letting him grab their bags and followed him toward the car.

"Can we stop for breakfast?" He called running a little to walk next to Derek.

He chuckled, "Yeah, we can do that."

Stiles smiled climbing into the front seat of the Camaro and slipping his shoes off to sit cross-legged on the seat. Derek climbed in after throwing their stuff in the trunk. "What're we gonna do about those packs...?"

"I don't know." Derek sighed starting the car. "Hopefully the Cambridge pack with just drop it now but I don't know how I'm supposed to convince Cora's old pack that she's safe with me."

"They can't just take her Derek. She's eighteen, she's an adult and can make her own decisions and she's not gonna leave you."

Derek shook his head, "Pack's will do whatever they think is necessary to get someone they want. Especially if they were once pack."

"We'll figure it out." Stiles replied grabbing onto Derek's hand. "OH! Der, Starbucks! Please!!!"

"You're such a pain." Derek laughed pulling into the parking lot and heading toward the drive-thru.

Stiles kissed the back of the other's hand, "But, you loooovvveee me." He teased.

"I do." Derek said glancing at him and looking back in front of them.

Stiles smiled, "I love you, too."

Derek smiled, "What do you want, angel?"

Stiles rolled his eyes, "Is that really gonna be a thing?"

Derek shrugged, smirk stitched to his face.

--

The pack all gathered in the living room when Stiles and Derek got home. Stiles had to make sure nothing happened while they were gone and when he was told that everything was fine his nerves dissipated.

"So, what're we gonna do?"

Derek rubbed his hand over his face letting Stiles pull him down into the armchair next to him and throw his legs over the wolf's lap. "I honestly don't know, Cor."

"What do you mean you don't know?" Isaac asked, "You're alpha, you're supposed to have a plan. You're supposed to know!"

"Is, calm down." Stiles snapped.

"He's just worried Stiles." Derek sighed.

Stiles crossed his arms, "I don't care. He doesn't need to talk to you like that."

"It's fine." Derek said,kissing the others cheek. "I don't know exactly what Cora's old pack wants so I don't have a plan. I'm sure we're just going to sit and talk, at least at first. We'll figure it out from there."

Isaac nodded, "What about Cambridge?"

"We shouldn't have to worry about them."

"Why not?"

Cora laughed, "Cause Derek claimed Stiles so now they can't have him."

"Wait, that's why you went off to do the mating ritual? So another pack couldn't take Stiles away?" Scott said.

"Scott it's not like that," Stiles started.

Scott shook his head, "No, he just did it to keep them away from you and now you're stuck together. Does he even love you?"

Derek growled, moving Stiles' off of him. His eyes glowing red as he stepped closer to Scott. "Don't you dare accuse me of not loving him. He's my mate."

"He better be." Scott snarled, Derek growled more pushing him against the wall.

"Derek!" Stiles snapped, Derek let Scott go.

"Don't ever think I would ask him to do something like that just to save this pack. I'd die before I forced him into anything he didn't want or I didn't truly feel."

Scott nodded, his gaze glued to Derek as Stiles squished between the two. "Fucking hell guys." He said, looking between both of them. He pushed Derek back, "Come on, Sourwolf! Move!"

Derek stopped Stiles, glancing at him, his facial features softening for a moment before he let go and made his way upstairs.

Stiles groaned, "I get you're my best friend and all but do you really think I'd fucking do something that serious with someone I wasn't serious about?"

"I don't know, Stiles!" Scott yelled, "You do a lot of stupid shit!"

Stiles shook his head, "If anyone shows up let me know." He said turning toward Cora and Isaac before following Derek upstairs.

Cora snorted, "You done fucked up," Scott rolled his eyes, "I'm serious Scott, talking to an alpha like that about his mate. Not good on your part. I'm surprised the only thing Derek did was shove you into the wall."

"I didn't do anything." Scott scoffed, "I'm just looking out for my best friend."

Cora shrugged, "I know Derek, I know he wouldn't do anything to hurt Stiles ever. He hasn't loved anyone this much since Paige."

"Yeah? And look how that turned out."

Cora growled, "I'm gonna fucking kill you."

Isaac grabbed Cora's arm, "Cora! Stop!" Cora fought against him, Boyd got up throwing her over his shoulder.

"It's not worth it Cora." Boyd turned to Scott, "Not cool."

Scott rolled his eyes walking away from the other three in the living room.

"What the hell is his problem?" Erica asked walking in with Lydia.

Isaac shrugged, "But he needs to get over himself before it's too late."

Chapter 27

<hr>

The pack was sitting at the table for breakfast the next morning when someone showed up. Cora was the first to get up, Derek following after when he realized it was her old pack. When they got outside the had realized only about a third of their pack had come, Derek visibly relaxing knowing that there wasn't going to be a fight today, at least not with them. A man, tan with half of his head shaven, the other half long and styled, stood in front of his pack, hands clasped together as if waiting for Derek to greet him. Derek stepped off of the porch nodding, his eyes flashing red, the other's flashing back.

"Where's your new mate?" Jamison asked.

Derek's posture stiffened, "He's inside."

Jamison nodded, "Congratulations."

"Thank you. But, you're not here to talk about my mate." Jamison nodded again. Derek nodded toward the house leading them inside.

Most of the pack was already sitting in the living room, getting up when Derek walked in with the other pack. Boyd and Jackson stayed seated as the others left like they were instructed to do the week prior. Stiles stood by the fireplace not quite sure if he should leave or not since the rules changed due to the mating ritual. Derek stared at Stiles, his eyes looking toward the love seat. Stiles sighed sitting down next to Cora as the alpha stood in front of them.

The other pack found seats, some of them choosing to stand against the wall behind their alpha. Jamison and Cora made small conversation before they decided to get down to business.

"She belongs with us."

Derek rolled his eyes, "She was only with you because she didn't know anyone in our family survived the fire."

"That's beside the point. She was pack to us and you weren't meant to be an alpha. She's not safe with you."

"Her safety is not your concern anymore."

The argument went on awhile longer before Stiles coughed and nervously got Derek's attention. The alpha tried to glare at him but wasn't able to keep the hard look on his face. Stiles waited for permission to speak.

"Let the boy speak, Hale." Jamison said, amusement lacing his voice.

Derek sighed, nodding, letting Stiles cling to his arm as he stood. "M-Maybe, we should just let Cora decide? She's been in b-both packs. She should know where she feels safest. I don't want her to leave b-but she's an adult now, she knows what's r-right for her."

Derek looked at Jamison, the room already knowing he was in agreement with his mate. Stiles mumbling an apology as he sat back down.

"No, that's a great idea. Cora, who do you want to be with?"

Cora looked between the two, "Look, Jamison, I love you and your pack so much and I'll always be grateful, but this is my family. Literally. I have my family back and I'm not leaving them no matter what."

Jamison nodded, "Alright. But don't expect a place in our pack in the future."

"I won't need one."

The other pack got up and left, Derek's body relaxing as Cora hugged him. "Love you big brother."

"Love you too, Cor."

He turned toward Stiles, "Don't apologize for speaking up."

Stiles nodded, "I-I didn't know if I was allowed to..."

"You're the alpha's mate. You have just as much of a say in things as he does now." Boyd mumbled from his seat.

Derek nodded, "We're equals."

Stiles nodded, "Okay."

Chapter 28

I t had been a few days and Derek had refused to talk to Scott after their argument. Stiles was over the petty drama between the two though and wanted to figure out a way to get them to talk everything out.

"What're you doing?" Isaac laughed seeing Stiles laying on his bed with his head upside down over the edge.

"Trying to teach myself how to dream walk." He said, red in the face.

"I'm not so sure that's going to work..."

Stiles flipped back over shrugging, "Probably not."

The two stood in silence for a minute, "I need my laptop." Stiles jumped up.

Isaac laughed again, "So, I have an issue..." Stiles raised his eyebrows, "I um...kinda like someone and I don't know what to do about it..."

Stiles began to chew on his nails, "I'm not sure I'm totally the best person to ask about relationship advice."

"I need more...Derek advice..."

Stiles scrunched his eyebrows again, "What do you mean?"

"I don't want him to hate me...but I don't want to tell him if nothings even gonna happen..."

Stiles sighed, realization smacking him as he nodded, "Scott and Allison are supposed to go to the movies later. Let me see if they'd be okay with you joining them."

"Okay, but what about De-"

"Just worry about how tonight goes first, I'll talk to Der."

Isaac got a panicked look on his face, "You're not actually gonna tell him ...right?"

Stiles snorted, "No."

--

The pack was sitting around the living room when Scott brought up what movie they were seeing later in the night.

"You guys are coming tonight right?" He asked.

Lydia looked up, "Coming where? Why wasn't I invited?"

"You can come Lyd. " Allison smiled, "We're going to the movies."

Lydia smiled, "ooo what're we seeing??"

"Please not a chick flick." Jackson groaned.

The front door shut, Derek walking in all sweaty. "Hi, Der!" Stiles yelled.

"Hi, babe." He said leaning over the couch to press a kiss to his cheeks. "What're you talking about?" He said slightly out of breath from his run.

"We're all going to the movies tonight." Cora mumbled.

"Since when?"

Stiles snorted, "No, we're not going."

"Why?"

Stiles raised his brows at the older male. "Oh. Okay." He smirked, heading toward the stairs.

The pale boy waited a minute before mumbling "I don't know what he's thinking but I'm eating tacos and watching Supernatural all night."

Scott laughed, "You're kind of an ass."

Stiles shrugged, "Don't have too much fun tonight!" He pushed himself off the couch, patting Isaac's shoulder as he walked passed.

--

"Hey Der...?" Stiles called while the two were getting ready for bed.

The wolf poked his head out of the doorway in their bathroom, toothbrush hanging out of his mouth, "Yeah?" he mumbled.

Stiles chuckled, "How would you feel if Cora started dating someone in the pack?"

"Why are you asking me that?" He said pulling the toothbrush out of his mouth, scowl stitched to his face.

"No real reason. Just curious." He said pulling one of Derek's t-shirts from the closet. "I mean it's probably bound to happen."

He pointed his toothbrush toward the younger, "You're not telling me everything. Who likes my baby sister?"

"Nobody!" He laughed.

Derek furrowed his brows ducking back into the bathroom to finish brushing his teeth. When he was finished he came up behind Stiles picking him up and throwing him onto the bed. The room filled with squeals of laughter from the younger as Derek started to tickle him.

"Stop!" Stiles wheezed, "I can't!" He tried rolling over, "I can't breathe!"

"Tell me and I'll stop."

"I promised!" Stiles started swatting at him.

Derek pined his arms down, "I'm not gonna stop until you tell me."

"I'm gonna pee Derek!" Stiles coughed around his laughter.

"Tell me!"

"Okay!!" Derek let Stiles go, the boy running to the bathroom. Derek heard a click right after the door shut.

"YOU'LL NEVER GET ME!"

Chapter 29

S tiles decided that since he planned on hiding in the bathroom for a while hoping Derek would either A.) Give up or B.) Fall asleep—probably the latter—he would take a nice long bath. He hummed to himself as he waited for the tub to fill up. It was probably his favorite part of the house. Derek had put in a beautiful claw foot tub that sat next to the glass encased shower. Stiles pulled out a candle from the closet and lit it before turning back to the closet to look through his collection of bath stuff. (Derek secretly would steal some bath bombs on occasion because "It's relaxing okay, leave me alone.") He made a happy noise finding one he liked and stripped dropping the bath bomb into the water. Bubbles exploded while pink and blue swirled around the water. "This was a good idea." He mumbled to himself.

He finally decided he should get out when he had started to doze off in the tub. He wasn't sure how long he'd been sitting in there but his fingers and toes were as pruned as they could possibly be. He dried off, pulled Derek's shirt back over his head and threw on his underwear before peeking through the doorway into the room. Derek was under the blanket, the TV playing quietly on the wall across from the bed. The wolf was laying on his stomach, arms wrapped tightly around his pillow, little snores filling the room. Stiles just smiled and shut off the light climbing into bed.

"Where am I?" Stiles mumbled to himself, walking up a dirt path. It led to his house. He scrunched his eyebrows together walking inside.

"Der?" He called.

"PAPA!" a little girl ran over to Stiles jumping up, hands way above her head. Stiles was confused but picked the little girl up letting her curl into him.

"Gabbie, I told you to leave your father alone, he just got home." Derek's voice came. "Hi, babe." He said pressing a kiss on his lips.

"What's going on?"

Derek scrunched his eyebrows, "What do you mean?" Stiles just shook his head, "Oh! Laura will be here soon with dessert for tonight. Your parents are on their way too."

"Wait what?"

Derek chuckled, "We're having pack night? Are you feeling okay?"

"Y-Yeah, I just forgot, I guess."

The wolf plucked the little girl from his arms. "Why don't you go shower before everyone else gets here."

"Okay."

"Roman is sleeping in our bed, he wasn't feeling great. Just try to be quiet."

"Who?"

Derek felt Stiles' forehead, "Your son?" He said, "Are you sure you're feeling okay?"

Stiles rubbed his hands over his face, "Maybe I should lay down."

Derek just nodded, "I'll see if mom has any tea left for you."

"Gramma!!" Gabbie yelled wiggling in Derek's arms.

"Your mom's here?"

"Yeah, she and dad have been cooking since you've been at work." Derek said, "Go lay down, I'll bring you tea."

Stiles nodded, Derek pressing a kiss to his cheek before he walked away. Stiles just shook his head and found his way into his and Derek's room. A little boy laying in the middle of the bed. He laid down next to him, he had Stiles' pale skin and Derek's dark brown hair, little moles all over the place. He looked down at his hands noticing the wedding band on his left ring finger. He smiled, whatever this was it was nice.

Stiles' eyes were heavy but he woke up when Derek moved next to him. "Sorry, did I wake you?"

The younger just shrugged, "What time is it?"

"About nine." Derek said, stretching his arms above his head.

"I had the best dream." Stiles hummed. "Our parents were here, and we had two kids."

Derek turned, his eyebrows scrunched up, "What?"

"My dream. We were having a pack night with our parents and our kids. Laura was coming. The pack was there..."

"Kids...?"

Stiles nodded, "Gabbie and Roman." The two said at the same time.

"Stiles. That was my dream too..."

He sat up in bed, looking at the wolf, "That's weird."

"Yeah..."

Stiles shrugged, "Maybe it's just some mate shit." He laughed.

"Probably..."

--

Stiles waited until Derek had left for his run before finding Isaac to ask how everything went last night.

"I like her, Stiles." He said, a small blush forming on his cheeks. "She said she wants to hang out again, just us."

Stiles smiled, "Good. I'm happy for you two."

"What about Derek? Did he say anything about...?"

Stiles shrugged, "I mentioned it and he just kept asking who liked her so I locked myself in the bathroom until he fell asleep."

Isaac chuckled, "Well...thanks."

"I'll ask some more." Stiles said. "But, he's gonna try to find out."

Isaac just nodded, "We'll see how tomorrow night goes first."

Stiles nodded leaving the room.

--

"So," Cora said, slightly out of breath as she stopped running. Derek came to a halt turning to face her.

"You okay?" He put his hands on his head.

Cora nodded, "I need to talk to you and you need to not freak out about it or on anyone or anything." Derek just nodded. "Promise me."

"I promise I won't freak out on anyone about what you tell me." Derek snorted rolling his eyes.

"You know how we went to the movies last night?" Derek nodded. "It was a double—kinda triple date."

Derek just raised his eyebrows at her, "But it was Scott and Allison, Lydia and Jackson, and..."

"Me and Isaac." She butted in.

"Oh."

"Are you mad?"

Derek bit his lip and shrugged. "I don't know."

"How do you not know?"

"Because I love Isaac and I know he'd never hurt you but I also hate the thought of you having a boyfriend and I'd still kill him if you get hurt but I don't want Isaac to get hurt either but...I don't know."

Cora snorted, "It's not actually anything yet. We don't know what's going on but I do think I like him and I don't want you freaking out and threatening him."

Derek nodded, "Well, if you guys like each other and he's respectful and doesn't hurt you, I'm fine with it."

"Not that you can control who I date." Cora muttered. "I figured you'd like to know from me before it just happens...if it does."

"Yeah, I'll still kill him."

Cora rolled her eyes, "Race ya."

"You're on."

Chapter 30

Derek was working on Stiles' Jeep when Scott and Isaac pulled into the driveway. They got out of the car laughing about something Derek couldn't care less about, Scott walking straight passed the older wolf into the house.

"Hey, Isaac?" Derek called, the curly haired boy stopped and turned toward him. The other could tell he seemed nervous when he glanced over, "Could you help me for a minute?"

"Y-Yeah, what do you need?"

"Can you just hold the flashlight? I can't do it and get this stupid thing."

Isaac nodded grabbing the flashlight and aimed it toward where Derek was working.

"Cora told me." Derek said softly.

"Oh."

"I'm not mad." Isaac let out a breath, "I love you both, but she's my little sister."

"Derek I-"

"I want both of you to be happy. If being with each other does that, I support it. But don't think I won't kill you if you hurt my baby sister."

Isaac just nodded, biting silently on his lip.

"She's cheesy. She likes stupid stuff in those lame movies Lydia watches all the time."

Isaac snorted, "You don't have to give me advice...I'm sure you don't want to."

"Just make her happy." Derek said with a slight nod, he grabbed the flashlight and shut the hood of the Jeep. "He's gonna destroy my bank account with this damn thing." He muttered more to himself.

"Rude." The two looked to see Stiles standing on the porch, "I always tell you I'll pay for it. You choose to take over." He said trying to scowl toward him.

"Yeah, yeah."

Isaac laughed, Derek wiping his hands on his pants. "Take her to Mooney's. It's her favorite." He said, patting Isaac on his shoulder and walking inside, pressing a kiss to Stiles' temple as he passed.

"I didn't tell him, I swear!" He raise his hands in surrender.

"I know." Isaac laughed, "Cora did, apparently."

"Is that bad?"

He shook his head, "No."

"Good. Good. Now I just have to get Derek and Scott talking again and everything will be fine."

"Good luck with that."

Stiles snorted, "Thanks."

--

"I'm getting a cat." Stiles mumbled sitting in bed next to Derek that night.

"You're what?"

"Getting a cat."

Derek set his book down, "Says who?"

"Me?"

"No."

Stiles snorts, "Der, I live here too. And I want a cat."

"We don't need a cat."

"I want one."

"Stiles..."

Stiles showed him a picture, "This one. Gizmo."

"No."

"Yup. I'm gonna go get him tomorrow." Stiles smiled looking at the picture again. "He's only a year."

"Why do you want a cat?"

Stiles shrugged, "Because they're cute and I can cuddle him."

"You can cuddle me."

"Not the same." Stiles set his phone on the bedside table. "Night, babe."

Derek watched the other lay down, pulling the blanket up to his nose. "You're not getting a cat."

"And if I do?"

"I'll beat you."

Stiles turned to look at him, "Kinky."

Derek rolled his eyes, "I hate you."

He hummed, "I don't think you do though."

Derek reached over and started tickling the younger, "I should."

Between his gasps for air and his laughter Stiles yelled out, "Stop!" repeatedly. Derek finally stopped pressing a kiss to his lips.

"Why didn't you tell me?" Stiles raised his eyebrows in confusion, "About Isaac and Cora?"

"I promised, Isaac. He didn't want to tell you unless it was for sure something they both wanted. And besides, not my business to tell."

Derek wrapped his arms around the younger, closing his eyes, "Still wish you had told me."

"Shut up, Sourwolf."

Derek chuckled, "I love you."

"I love you too."

Chapter 31

"**H**ey, Derbear." I sang walking into Derek's office. Derek hummed from his desk not looking up at me from the papers in front of him. "I think it's about time you and Scott talk."

"No thanks."

"Please, Bear?" I moved to sit in his lap. "I'm just as angry about what he said as you but he's pack and you guys need to sort this out."

"He's only still here because of you."

"Oh shut up, you love him like he's a brother."

Derek sighed, wrapping his arms around my waist, "What do I get out of this?"

I raised my eyebrow, "What do you want?"

He sat silently for a moment, "I really want pizza."

I snorted, "We can have pizza."

He smiled pressing his lips against mine. "I love you."

"I love you, too."

--

"Where is everyone?" Scott asked as I set the pizza box on the kitchen table.

"What're you talking about?"

"You said there's a pack meeting? There's nobody here?"

I scrunched my eyebrows together, "I said we need to meet."

"Same thing?"

I watched Derek walk into the kitchen, pressing a kiss to my cheek before grabbing some plates out of the cupboard. "I'm surprised you actually got him here."

"Seriously, why am I here?"

I took a plate from Derek, grabbing some pizza and a few wings before turning back to my best friend, "Because you two assholes need to sort your shit out."

Scott rolled his eyes, "There's nothing to sort out." Derek huffed a snort, pulling out pizza for himself. "How'd you even get him here?"

"I live here, Scott."

"You know that's not what I meant."

"He wants to have my babies, so he does things for me." I replied, sitting in the chair next to Derek. "Please, Scotty?"

Scott sighed, dropping into a chair with a groan. I handed him a plate with pizza on it, seeing him take it begrudgingly.

The two didn't bother speaking a single word as they ate. I glanced back and forth between them a few times. "Do I seriously have to do everything?"

"What the hell do you want me to say?" Scott snapped.

Derek growled toward the other, "Relax, Derek." I turned toward Scott, "I don't know, maybe apologize?"

"For worrying about you?"

"For being an asshole." Derek interrupted. "I seriously can't believe you would fucking accuse me of-" He stopped, letting out a harsh laugh.

"I wouldn't have said it if I didn't have a reason."

"But that's it, Scott. You had no reason. You'd been bugging me repeatedly about coming clean to Stiles for months. So, I finally fucking do and you accuse me of only doing it to keep him in the pack?"

I looked at Derek, "Wait, he what?"

"Yeah, and then out of nowhere you guys just rush off to do the mating ritual as there is a threat out against us." Scott ignored me.

"Because he's my mate and I love him! I told him if he didn't want to we didn't have to."

"Stiles is a pushover!" Scott yelled, "He hates telling people no!"

"I know when he's lying!" Derek snapped.

Scott rolled his eyes, "you and me both know he has learned to steady his heart beat."

"Scott, he literally can't lie to me."

"I know you're the alpha. But Stiles is Stiles."

Derek took a deep breath, "I'm not saying that. He literally can't lie to me, he gets this stupid little grin on his face and his cheeks get red and he swears he's telling the truth and all I do is look at him and he breaks. He hasn't lied to me since..."

"My dad..." I said quietly, looking at Derek who now had ahold of my hand.

Everyone was quiet for a long time before I excused myself. Thinking about my dad still hurts. A lot. And I know I can see him whenever but just like Derek said, it's not the same as actually having him with me.

Derek POV

"I'm sorry." Scott said softly, "I didn't realize..."

"Didn't realize what?"

"How serious this whole thing between you guys is."

"Scott, I love him. So fucking much. And you of all people should know the last thing I do is put my wants first." I sighed, "If he didn't feel it too I wouldn't have even told him he's my mate."

Scott nodded, "You're right. What I said was really messed up, I get if you don't forgive that. But I'm sorry."

I nodded, "I should check on him."

When I found Stiles he was sitting in his room looking through a photo album, I sat down next to him.

"I really miss them." He said softly.

"I know you do."

He closed the book, setting it beside him. "Do I really do all that when I lie to you?"

I nodded, feeling a smile on my face, "Yeah, you do."

"I didn't realize you noticed things like that."

"I notice everything to do with you."

Stiles leaned into me, "I love you."

"I love you,

Chapter 32

S tiles sighed, contently, laying across the hot surface of the cliff he was on. Lydia and Isaac were nearby. Lydia had packed a picnic for the three of them and suggested they come here so Stiles could stretch out his wings for a while.

"How's it going with Cora?" He asked, eyes closed.

"Good." Isaac started, "We're going out later. Taking her to Mooney's like Derek suggested."

"Nice, she loves it there."

"Get her flowers." Lydia chimed in, looking at her nails.

"OOOO!" Stiles shouted, sitting up, "This means the house will be empty tonight!"

"Ew." Isaac laughed.

Stiles rolled his eyes, "I'm trying to convince Derek to let me get a kitten. So, I think I can just sneak one in tonight and give him my little puppy eyes and then he'll be fine with it."

"Awh, I love Kittens. And Derek's such a pushover when it comes to you, you could get twelve and he'd pretend to be mad before giving you that look and saying 'fine I guess we can keep them'." Lydia laughed.

Stiles shrugged, "He's squishy, he just pretends he's not."

Lydia laughed, "If you're gonna fly around, you should. Pack will be headed over soon for the meeting."

The other male just nodded, sitting up to stretch a bit before letting his wings out. "Still so weird." Isaac murmured, getting a laugh from Stiles.

They watched their friend fly around for a bit, coming above them and over the edge of the cliff. It had only been a few minutes before he came spiraling down to the ground landing on his wing. He screamed, Lydia dropping down by his side, "I got you, I'll call Deaton."

"I want Derek." He muttered in between his sobs.

Isaac didn't hesitate before howling loudly, knowing Derek would respond faster to that than a call. He heard a short howl back, dropping next to Stiles to take some of his pain. Derek was there and by Stiles' side in minutes pulling his pain.

"Babe, what happened?"

"Someone popped out of nowhere and I ran into them."

"Stiles, nobody was there?" Isaac stated, confusion laced between his words.

Stiles shook his head, "An angel. He's gone."

Derek growled a bit as Stiles let out another cry. "Deaton is almost here." Lydia said softly.

Stiles was patched up shortly after and Deaton told him he would have to leave his wing out in order for it to heal. He sighed, leaning into Derek's side.

"What exactly happened?"

"There was someone there, clearly I could only see him. It was an angel. He popped up literally like seconds before I hit him and I fell."

"I'm gonna kill him." Derek growled.

"It was an accident."

"They didn't even stick around to see if you were okay, Stiles!" Isaac snapped.

"Yeah, probably because I have two crazy eyed werewolves all pissed off next to me."

Derek grunted, "I'm going to kill whoever this ass is."

"Der, relax. I'm sure it wasn't on purpose."

"I don't care." He growled back.

"U-um hi. I'm so sorry. I didn't mean to bump into you."

Everyone turned to see a short guy with light blonde hair standing a few feet away, he had piercing green eyes and was clearly full of guilt and anxiety.

"Who are you?" Stiles asked before anyone else had time to speak up.

"I uh, I'm Gus. I was sent to check on you." nerves laced his words, strangling his voice. "I really didn't mean for that to happen. I was just trying to pop in, see how you were, and be on my way. You normally don't even know I'm here, clearly I made a mistake in my trajectory."

"Clearly." Stiles muttered to himself, "wait, normally? How long have you been spying on me?"

"Spying? No, no. I don't think I'd call it that. Really I'm just doing my job."

"Which is to what? Spy on me." Stiles asked, Derek pulling him closer into his side.

Gus sighed, "I'm just sent to make sure you're doing okay, ya know, like.." He pointed to his head. "It's not uncommon for Guardians to get kinda. ..ehh up there."

"Who the hell is even telling you to check in on me?" He scoffed, "Jesus?"

Gus rolled his eyes, "He's a fraud. The Gods, plural, like to be kept in the loop though."

"Gods?" Isaac butted in.

Gus nodded, "Zues, Hera, Athena. You know them."

"You're serious?" Disbelief fell across Stiles, "If they're all real and want to know how I am, why haven't I ever met them?"

The other angel laughed, "dude, they're busy. Like all the time. You need to wait your turn to meet them. I only know them because I'm working for them as your guardian basically."

"Why do I need a guardian?"

"Because guardians don't look out for themselves. That's why."

Stiles scoffed, "Whatever. Next time don't pop up literally right in front of me. And maybe stop lurking in the shadows like you have something to hide. Also, I don't believe you and if you're telling the truth then I want to meet these bastards."

With an exaggerated sigh Gus answered, "I'll see what I can do."

"Now I can't sneak a kitten into the house." Stiles pouted.

"We're not getting a cat." Derek muttered, Gus disappearing.

"Clearly not, I can't go anywhere until my stupid wing heals and by then Gizmo will be gone."

"Babe." The pack stared silently at Derek.

Stiles just sighed, "Can we just go home now, my wing hurts."

—

"Babe!" Derek called walking into the house the next afternoon. "Stiles?"

"I'm playing video games, what?"

"I got you something." He replied carrying a box into the living room.

Stiles smiled, tossing the controller onto the couch, "A present? For me??" He grabbed the box feeling a hole on the side. "You shut up."

Derek smirked, nodding toward the box. "Open it."

Stiles pulled off the top revealing a Siamese kitten, curled into a ball asleep. "Is it Gizmo?"

"It's Gizmo."

Chapter 33

Stiles groaned as he sat on the floor of the living room, wings spread wide, playing with a wand above Gizmo's head. It had only been a couple days since he injured his wing, but he still had until Friday before he could retract them and to say he was bored of being stuck at home was an understatement.

"You literally only have the rest of today and tomorrow babe, you will be okay."

That only made Stiles groan even louder, "HOW can you act like this is nothing. I'm so bored, Der!"

Derek chuckled, "We can go do absolutely anything you want on Friday, okay?" Stiles just pouted.

—

Friday came and Derek held true to his word asking Stiles what he wanted to do. He said he wanted to go to a club "and not the Jungle, I'm so sick of that place." he muttered. Which is how they ended up here, at a club two towns over that Derek knew would spike the drinks to let the pack have a good time.

They picked out a few bar tables, Derek left the pack to head up to the bar. "What can I get you handsome?"

"I have a group, three tables." He nodded, "Can you just do aconite shots with everything?"

The bartender nodded with a smirk, "Sounds good to me." She said, as Stiles came up from behind.

"I'll get a top shelf whiskey, neat. He wants something fruity that you can't taste any liquor."

"Rude." Stiles muttered, Derek raised his brows to the younger, "Okay you're not wrong but still."

She smiled softly at the two, "Congrats." she nodded. Stiles scrunched his brows as Derek thanked her.

"Why'd she say congrats?" He asked on the way back to the table, Sipping on his drink. Derek pressed lightly onto the claim mark resting where Stiles' shoulder and neck meet. It sent a shiver through his body, "Oh."

Derek watched Stiles have fun with his packmates most of the night, they didn't do too much other than talk and drink, occasionally dancing together. Stiles and Erica were currently the only ones on the dance floor. Derek watched them, leaning back in his chair. He only had a couple drinks and then switched to water as well as Jackson, the two being the ones to drive everyone. He watched Stiles pull away from Erica and walk back toward the bar, setting his empty glass down. He could hear Jackson saying something to him, Scott and Isaac also contributing to the conversation. Stiles was only at the bar for a couple minutes, chatting with the bartender when some guy who looked as if he stepped out of a teen drama as the quarterback came up behind him, placing a hand on his back. Stiles moved away but greeted the newcomer, Derek felt the growl in his throat rising.

"Derek?" Jackson muttered, clearly annoyed, before turning to follow the alphas gaze, "Oh."

Derek pushed himself up and planted himself beside Stiles, pulling the younger further from the other guy. "You should fuck off."

The other snorted, "And you are?"

"He's-" Stiles started, getting cut off by Derek.

"His husband."

Stiles' eyes shot over to Derek, a smile forming on his face.

"I don't see a ring."

Derek shrugged, "Not yet, but I know you're not dumb enough to not notice this." He snapped, pushing Stiles' shirt collar a bit more, exposing the claim, eyes flashing red.

The stranger's eyes flashed back gold and sighed, irritation filling the room, "my bad."

"Fuck off."

Stiles waited until the other wolf walked away, "Husband huh?" he nudged into Derek.

Derek just ordered another whiskey, protectively wrapping an arm around Stiles' waist. He downed the drink and turned to Stiles, "Yeah, start planning."

"Did you just ask me to marry you in the worst way possible?" He laughed.

"I'll take you to pick out a ring tomorrow."

Stiles smiled, "Fine, but I expect a real proposal, husband."

—

They looked at rings the next day. For whatever reason Derek didn't expect Stiles to be picky. But he was. Very.

"What if we get the wrong ones?"

"How would they be the wrong ones?"

"Like," Stiles sighed, "What if we end up hating them?"

Derek rolled his eyes, "Then we'll get new ones."

"What!? NO. These ones will mean something Derek." Stiles scoffed. "They're not just going to be some normal jewelry you could get any day of the year for whatever reason."

"Then, we'll get new ones when we renew our vows."

That made Stiles beam, "We're gonna renew our vows?"

"Every year."

"Okay."

—

After picking out their rings and placing the order for the two with the right sizes to be made and shipped the two ended up just spending a few days together. It was like the pack just decided that the pair needed alone time and didn't seem to bother coming around. Derek had set up a picnic for the two of them that next Saturday, finding a nice clearing in the preserve.

They ate and laid on the grass looking up at the clouds together, silence filling the space comfortably. Stiles stretched his left hand up above him looking at his finger, imagining what it would be like to wear a ring every day. It wasn't like they weren't already kind of married, but just knowing that Derek actually wanted to marry him? Have a wedding? It made him all warm and fuzzy inside and he couldn't help to think about what else they would do.

Dropping his hand he turned onto his stomach, "So..."

"So...?" Derek mocked, turning his head to look at the other.

"I, um, was wondering..." He paused, biting on his lip. "Do you want kids?"

"Now?" Derek raised his eyebrows in shock.

"No." Stiles snorted, "I mean, unless you want to and then we can talk about it!"

Derek smiled fondly, "I do want kids, just not yet."

He got a smile in return, "Me too." It was quiet again for a moment, "How would we...?"

"Well, that depends, we could adopt. Or get a surrogate."

Stiles nodded, silence wrapping around his head, and drifting into the sky, "What about the whole werewolf thing?"

"What about it?"

"Would it be better to have a supernatural kid?"

Derek shrugged, "I don't think it's any better than having a human kid." He sat up, "There are agencies we can use that can help us if you want a werewolf baby."

"I never thought I'd be asking my husband," He started, making Derek laugh, "if he wants human children or werewolf children."

"Me either."